this place

that place

this place

NANDITA
DINESH

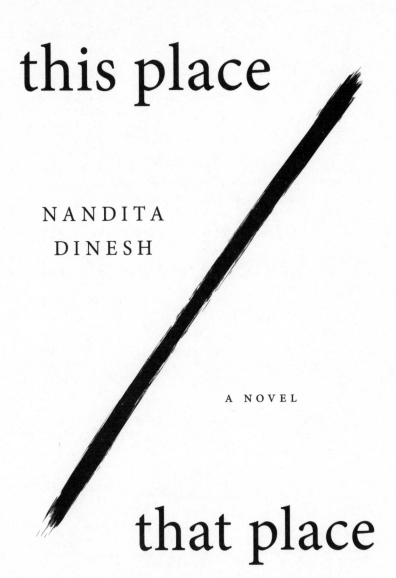

A NOVEL

that place

MELVILLE HOUSE
BROOKLYN · LONDON

THIS PLACE, THAT PLACE

Melville House Publishing
46 John Street
Brooklyn, NY 11201

and

Melville House UK
Suite 2000
16/18 Woodford Road
London E7 0HA

mhpbooks.com
@melvillehouse

ISBN: 9781612199498
ISBN: 9781612199504 (eBook)

Library of Congress Control Number: 2022933938

Designed by Beste M. Doğan

Printed in the United States of America
1 3 5 7 9 10 8 6 4 2

A catalog record for this book is available from the Library of Congress

For Hritik,
and all the conversations that will
have to be imagined.

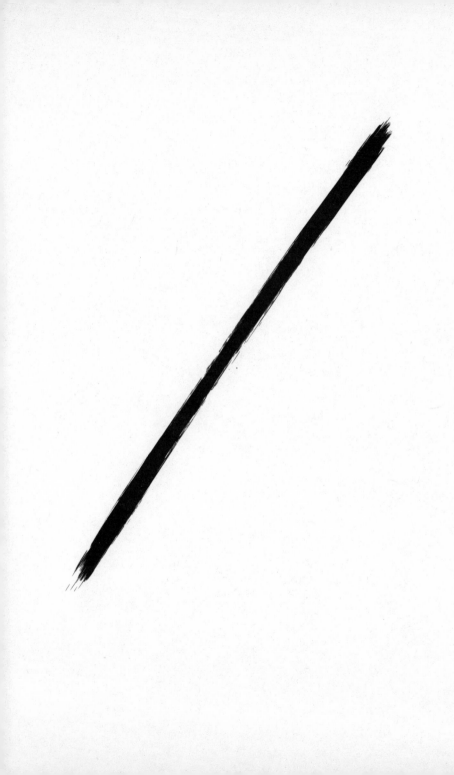

◆ I can't believe that man.

▪ What else can you expect? He's been perfectly transparent about his attitude toward us since the election.

◆ Impetuous, I think they call it.

▪ What?

◆ Him. His actions. I think the word for it is 'impetuous.' You know, like . . . authoritarian . . . or doing something without thinking through the consequences.

▪ Those are different things.

◆ What?

▪ Authoritarian. Or doing something without thinking through the consequences.

◆ I know they're different things, I'm just saying what I think the word means.

▪ Impetuous?

◆ Yes.

- Yeah, maybe.

◆ Maybe what?

- Maybe that's what it is.

◆ What?

- Him! Maybe impetuous is the right word to describe what he's done.

◆ Right. Well, it doesn't really matter what the word is, I suppose. He is . . . who he is.

- Insightful.

\ \ \ \ \ \ \

- It makes me so mad that he is doing this in my name. In *our* name. It's a fucking disgrace.

◆ I know.

- It's just this is . . . so typical. This mentality. That Place knows what's good for This Place. He knows what's good for an entire region and people. Un-fucking-believable.

◆ It was only a matter of time. The signs were all there. The increased number of troops, the veiled language, the vilification in the media, the increased number of lynch mobs. We knew it was coming.

- What's going to happen now?

◆ What always happens during a curfew. They'll shut everything down. The internet. The television channels. The shops. The roads. They'll do their best to keep us locked inside our homes, isolated from the world. They'll increase the number of troops on the streets. They'll suspend, in the name of security, laws that guarantee us some semblance of human rights. But they know. They know that their shutdown will lead to one eventuality. A protest. A shit-ton of protests . . . which means I'm about to get real busy real soon.

■ How will you coordinate everything without being able to communicate?

◆ Each neighbourhood has a spot where people gather at a specific time on days like today. The spots and times shift every week. I just need to look at the calendar and figure out where and when we'll be meeting this week. Actually, let me find that right now.

She looks out the window. She loves looking out windows when she is in This Place, because its landscape is so radically different from everything she has ever known. The rugged mountains. The architecture of the homes. Even the light. All of it feels different here.

The light in This Place feels like glitter. A glitter that seems to contain glinting particles that could blind a person. Particles that seem to ebb and flow like the waves in the sea. This is not the kind of thing that she has seen in her home, That Place. There, the light isn't like glitter. There, the light feels more like a haze.

It's almost as if the glitter speaks to the mood of This Place. When things are tense, the particles seem sharper somehow. Like they are made of powdered glass. At other times, when things are good, the glitter has an aura—an illusion that allows the gazer to lose themselves in a shimmery nothingness of optimism and hope, both of which are scarce commodities.

She knows she sees This Place and its glitter through the rose-tinted glasses of someone from That Place, someone who doesn't have to deal with its realities on a daily basis, someone who is predisposed to seeing This Place as, somehow, being "more" than That Place. She knows that she stands the risk of exoticizing This Place by focusing on things like the glitter, if she does not simultaneously pay sufficient attention to the rough edges and shards that underlie it. She knows that narratives about the magical glitter are easy to sell. The narratives of the rough shards, not so much.

As she looks out the window, she sees the shimmering shards of glass that, today, are reflecting ominous undertones. A changed Guarantee that now annexes This Place to That Place without question or consensus or debate or dialogue. A changed law that has transformed occupation into colonialism. Or colonialism into occupation. Whichever one better communicates the idea that today, things in This Place have gone from bad to much, much worse.

Today, she sees something else in the glitter. Something that she has never seen before. Not once in the twenty-four nonconsecutive months spanning seven years that she has spent in This Place, has she seen this particular quality to the glitter. Today, there is something in the particles that she finds disconcerting. Something that makes her scared. Something like . . . it's hard to explain. Something that is more menacing and unnerving than the shard-like edges she has seen before. Something that is more . . . charged.

■ Ok, so here. Look. That's the meeting place and time for tomorrow.

◆ Are you sure you should be showing that to me?

Oh, fuck. Yes. No. I shouldn't. Sorry. ■

◆ Right.

Forget you ever saw that. ■

◆ Right.

I'm so used to y—you're like family now. Sometimes I forget that you're not from here. ■

◆ You never forget that I'm not from here.

I didn't mean— ■

◆ It's okay. I never forget that I'm not from here either.

\ \ \ \ \ \ \

- I can't believe it happened today, of all days.

♦ This is not what you want to happen on your wedding day.

- No. It isn't.

When she is not looking out the window, she watches him play the snake game on his phone. A ritual she knows he follows during curfew. It's his way of changing time-gears. Of preparing himself for a clampdown that has no determined end-time. So, like most of the first hours of most of the curfews that he has had to experience in his life, she watches him play the game to prepare himself for the shitstorm that he knows is coming.

She watches him play the game as a way to think-without-thinking about the logistics that he will have to pull together before heading to tomorrow's meeting and helping orchestrate what happens next. He moves the snake around the screen, gobbling down blobs of light. And as the pixelated snake gobbles other pixelated blobs of light, the reptile's body becomes longer and more unwieldy. But even though the snake increases in length and, in so doing, consumes more blobs of light, its increasing size is the very thing that makes the snake more likely to crash into the pixelated walls and borders of that phone-sized world. Because, you see, in the world of the snake, the blobs of light are placed in and around barriers. Therefore, zig-zagging the ever-longer snake around the barriers so that it can consume more blobs of light, becomes a more arduous task (well, 'arduous' for a game on a phone that is being used to pass the time). Oh, and if the snake hits any of the walls or borders, it explodes. And the player needs to start over. The game transfixes him.

She watches him watch the snake swerve and dance through the walls and borders. She watches him watch the snake gobble blobs of light and grow longer and longer and longer and longer and longer each time. Sometimes the snake rams into a wall and bursts into pixelated flames. At which point she watches him hit 'restart' and begin the snake's journey all over again. She knows that he finds the snake game cathartic, somehow. Hopeful, even. That snake. Trying to consume blobs of light that it doesn't understand so that it can get longer, only so that it can risk bashing into a wall and decimating its own existence.

She knows that, for him, the snake game is inseparable from curfew. When the phone lines go down, and the internet is turned off with no known date of return, the snake game is one of the first things on his to-do list. He has played this game so many times and yet, each time—during each new curfew—he finds the snake to be endlessly fascinating. Its greed. Its consumption. And its eventual self-destruction.

1:57 PM

◆ How long do you think it'll be?

▪ Who knows. An hour. A few hours. A day. More. You know how it is.

◆ I hope it's not more than a few hours . . .

▪ The bodies haven't started dropping yet. As soon as they do, and as soon as word starts getting out about the inevitable casualties, we're fucked. There's no way the fighters are going to stay off the streets then. And . . . well, it's all downhill from there, isn't it? If we're really, really lucky, it'll be a few hours. But if my read on this situation is correct, this . . . this is going to be bad. Perhaps the worst yet. Worse than we know to expect. This . . . this could last for months.

Months. This could last for months. It's not like he wasn't used to it. He was. As used to it as any person could be. But even someone with his curfew practice was used to a couple of weeks at the most. Months would be daunting. Even for him. He wanted to hope against hope that he was exaggerating, that he was overstating the removal of the Guarantee.

And yet, even in the first half hour of this curfew, he could feel the difference. This time was different like every time was different, sure. But this time felt like a change in the course of history. A change in the course of possibility. This curfew didn't feel like a violent roadblock in one community's struggle for freedom. This curfew felt like a bomb had exploded and destroyed an entire people's vision for their future.

The Guarantee was the last remaining legal document that shone a beacon of hope for This Place. The only remaining tangible, internationally recognized law that bolstered the case for This Place's autonomy. With the Guarantee revoked, That Place could now do whatever they wanted. Whenever they wanted. With absolute impunity. Even more than they already did.

As he thought more about it, his forecast of a months-long curfew didn't seem like an exaggeration or an overstatement. Although he first uttered 'months' almost flippantly, with a 'let's see how you respond to the intensity of my life' kind of provocation toward her, he was coming to believe his own poorly intentioned prophecy. He couldn't stop himself from fucking with people from That Place by saying things like that. Forcing upon them a fear that he wore like a second skin.

If push came to shove though, if he would have to live under curfew for months, he didn't know what he would do. What he could do. His work would intensify. More protests. More events. More designs. More fighting. But there would also be a lot more sitting around at home with nothing really to be done. More boredom. More lack of communication. More sobs. More timeless(ness). More grazing. More glazing. More genie-ing. More glorification. More gazing. More glowing. More grooming. *More—stop. Stop going down this rabbit hole. Today is your brother's wedding day. Today was supposed to be your brother's wedding day. Today, all you think about should be related to him and his bride-to-be. Today should be about them.*

It's not about you.

It's not about you. It's not about you.

It's not about you. It's not about you. It's not about you.

It's not about you. It's not about you.

It's not about you.

As he repeated this mantra to himself, he could feel her scepticism from across the room. He could feel her consider the possibility of his being hyperbolic. He knew that she'd only ever experienced a curfew for a couple of days. That while a few days—maybe even a week—was in the realm of her imagination, months . . . ? That was an idea that she couldn't begin to conceive of.

Months. Months of sitting around in rooms. With no internet. No working mobile phones. Limited access to the world outside the doors of your home. No. There's no way this could happen for months. Not in her imagination.

◆ It's their wedding.

▪ Yes. Yes, it is.

◆ This shouldn't happen on someone's wedding day.

▪ No. It shouldn't.

He thought about quitting multiple times a day. And most of the time, these thoughts coincided with the moment he lit the next cigarette he held between his fingers. But it was like he couldn't help himself. He would take a drag of the cigarette and find himself blissfully yet guiltily ignoring his thoughts of quitting the habit. He would find himself savouring the ritual—the addiction—that he couldn't stop feeling guilty about. The kind of guilty pleasure that cannot be explained to someone who doesn't know it.

He hated the smell of it. He really didn't like having the smell of cigarette smoke on his hair, his fingers, his clothes. But taking a drag of that cigarette . . . it just helped. It helped calm him down. It helped him appreciate the glitter again.

Maybe that was an excuse. Maybe this line of thinking simply allowed him to use the cigarette as a crutch. To keep using it even when he knew the things that all smokers know when they pick up the habit and continue it and continue to continue it . . .

He knew the risks. Every time he thought about quitting, he would read about the risks. He would study the statistics. He would try to absorb the information into the core of his being, so that he could quit. And, every week, at least once, he thought that—this time—the information had stuck. That this time, it would be different. That this time, his brain really understood the risks and would make the decision to quit.

Despite understanding the risks though, he thought about his addiction as being part of a larger question surrounding his philosophical approach to life. Is longevity really the goal? Or does living a life mean doing things that make the everyday more bearable? If he got sick, he'd just shoot himself, to cut out the suffering and the pain and physical and mental degradation. So, in the time that he had left, did he really want to give up a habit that brought him relief, so that he could live for more time in a truly fucked up world? Wasn't his mortality already in jeopardy every day, regardless of the cigarette in his hands? Wasn't he just as likely to be shot by soldiers while he crossed the street as he was of developing a smoking-related disease? Didn't simply living in This Place raise his odds of never returning home on a given day? So, if he was probably going to die young anyway, might as well have his cigarettes, no?

It was almost a rite of passage for him, smoking. He had been given his first cigarette by his mother, during a curfew. A particularly poignant curfew in which a particularly life-altering story had been shared. A story about a soldier, a young woman, and a conception that took place in the most devastating of circumstances. A story that he knew he would have to—that he wanted to—share with the woman sharing this curfew with him . . . On that curfewed night, sharing a cigarette, mother and son had found some solace—an association with the habit that made it even more difficult for him to leave it behind. Even now, as he puffed the thing in between his fingers, he felt just a little bit calmer. Like things might actually be ok.

It wasn't all memory-based though. Like many people who smoke, he felt like a badass when he had the thing between his fingers. Utterly ridiculous notion, intellectually, but years of conditioning from different sources had succeeded in making him believe this acknowledged ridiculousness. He felt more radical because he smoked. He was dying faster with every puff, sure. But he was also dying looking pretty damn cool. Who didn't want that?

As he took the last puff of this one, he thought about the last cigarette that he had smoked with his brother. Which was right before the phone call from the bride's fathers, telling them to delay their departure because there was already unrest brewing on the streets of their neighbourhood. Which was right before the announcement that was broadcast on the radio that a curfew had officially been declared and that no one in the city was allowed to leave their homes unless they had a curfew pass for a medical emergency. Which was right before the news alert that the Leader of That Place had decided to revoke the Guarantee that gave This Place special status until issues surrounding its nationhood were resolved.

Sometimes, they could get curfew passes for weddings. But that depended on the gravity of the curfew and why it was being imposed. For a curfew like this one, it was unlikely that passes would be given for weddings . . . The curfew pass was a precious commodity in This Place and obtaining one depended on one's connections. Who you knew. What strings you could pull. How much you could pay. Luckily for them, the bride's family was well-connected. Maybe they could make some calls. Maybe they could get the elusive and highly sought-after pass? While a part of him fervently wished that strings would be pulled on his brother's behalf, another part already hoped that the wedding would be postponed. He didn't want his brother to forever remember his wedding day as the day when This Place had every ounce of its autonomy, whatever little it possessed, taken away. That's not the kind of thing anyone in This Place would want to remember.

He watched her look outside the window. Was she thinking about the wedding? She had told him once that she had never been much of a believer in the institution of marriage, or what it represented. Not for any lack of romance, or any fear of commitment, or the reasons that are usually associated with those who choose to self-partner. No. She had told him that she just didn't understand the notion of two people sticking together for the rest of their lives, regardless of how both of them might change and evolve and coalesce and fracture in the future. She had told him that she couldn't fathom how a promise made on one day could be expected to last an eternity. She had said then that she thought of a marriage as committing to a lifetime, based on limited information. Limited information that—while not necessarily withheld or misrepresented intentionally—is limited by a life that has only been lived until the day of the marital commitment. "How can anyone make such a promise, in good faith?" she had asked him then.

And yet, despite her statements questioning the promise that so many accept as an integral marker of a person's maturity into adulthood, he knew her to be a romantic. The kind of romantic who believed in possibility even when happily ever afters seemed unlikely. The kind of romantic who could critically pick apart the institutions that govern love yet believe, fiercely, in bonds that could remain untainted by the slightest hint of artifice. The kind of romantic who didn't believe in marriage herself but could feel unfettered empathy for today's bride and groom.

He knew that her opinion about marriage made her a pariah amongst most people in This and That Place. People in These Places weren't supposed to question such things. They were not supposed to question something so fundamental as marriage. And perhaps it was this rule-breaking quality to her questioning that made her more prone to doing it. Sure, she questioned marriage because questioning convention came naturally to her. But she also questioned marriage because it delighted her that she was doing something that was traditionally unexpected. It made her feel . . . rebellious. Avant-garde. Radical. She liked defining herself in that way. He knew that.

◆ It's their wedding day.

▪ Yes. I get it. It's their wedding day.

◆ It's not supposed to be like this.

▪ Well . . . they'll just reimagine what it's supposed to be like. We've become good at that.

◆ What?

▪ Reimagination. Reimagining things. It's a muscle we've had to develop.

2:27 PM

They stayed quiet for a while. Just sitting together in silence. Listening to music waft in from downstairs. A love song from an old romantic film. Tones that encapsulated how the entire household felt at that moment. Like unrequited love. Like nostalgia.

When no words were spoken, it was easier for them to forget that even the shapes of their words were often different.

When no words were spoken, it was easier for them to imagine a world in which they both inhabited the same side of the page.

WHERE IT BEGAN

When the Empire collapsed, This Place's rulers-at-the-time made an ill-advised move to ask for That Place's help in a complete overreaction to the overtures made by the Other Place. After all, didn't the Other Place make the attempt to enter This Place because so many of the latter's citizens wanted to be annexed to the former? How could the event be called an invasion when a majority of This Place-ers wanted the Other Place's support and only the ruling class didn't?

That Place had commandeered a tenuous situation and taken advantage of an already misguided invitation/request made by This Place's rulers-at-the-time. And as a consequence of this misstep, conditions of occupation/colonialism/neocolonialism were created. As a direct result of That Place's greed and megalomania.

In its power grab, That Place went beyond what was originally stated in the agreement between This Place and That Place: a temporary offer of resources from the latter to the former to help This Place make its way through a particular time of social and political upheaval. However, instead of respecting the terms of that agreement and leaving This Place when the necessary assistance had been provided and the upheaval in question calmed, That Place simply stayed. They annexed This Place, against the will of most of its citizens. "You are part of our Empire now," they said. "You have no choice in the matter, unless we say so." And just like that, That Place occupied This Place and forcefully imposed its nationhood upon it. "You have nothing to worry about," That Place had had the audacity to say. "What's more, we'll even bestow a Guarantee, which ensures that you can never make a decision about your autonomy without our consent. But don't worry, this Guarantee also means that we acknowledge your special identity. The Guarantee symbolises the fact that you are different from every other region that forms part of our Empire. You, This Place, *you* are special. And we're going to make sure you know that, one way or the other."

And as a response to this series of events, This Place saw the rise of an entire generation of revolutionary groups. Some of these groups had been created and trained and funded and developed by the Other Place. Interestingly, some of these revolutionary groups were said to have been created and trained and funded and developed by That Place—as one more way to get their agenda to take root in This Place. The best way to take down a revolution, after all, is from the inside. A handful of these groups were undoubtedly homegrown, indigenous, driven entirely by children of This Place's soil.

Initially, all the revolutionary groups had done their best to adopt nonviolent modes of resistance. They organised protests and sit-ins and hunger strikes and petitions and conferences and cultural exchanges and diplomatic dialogues. But slowly, over the course of two decades, when none of these efforts seemed to produce any results whatsoever, a rift emerged. A rift that created multiple subgroups of revolutionary groups. Subgroups that believed things had reached a point where violence had become necessary. Other subgroups that still believed in nonviolent, creative modes of resistance. More subgroups that thought it was time to call it quits and accept their fate as part of That Place.

That Place did its best to quash these revolutionaries (well, those who weren't funded by it). While more-evolved governments might have seen this upsurge in revolutionary subgroups as a strong indicator that things needed to change, that perhaps the relationship between This and That and the Other Place had to shift, nothing of the kind happened. Instead, That Place seemed to want to underscore its position as the most ruthless and feared nation in the world. If their government had had any compassion or integrity, That Place would have simply cut off This Place from its national entity and allowed its citizens to decide its fate.

That Place's departure will not solve This Place's issues. Over the years so many different views on This Place's status have taken root that, even if the occupation ended, This Place would have a lot to figure out. Ideally, what is needed is a political solution in which That Place leaves our land, but with a careful plan for transition that is developed in close collaboration with leaders of This Place and the Other Place.

But of course, That Place would never let something like that happen. They had/have/will always have too much to gain from this occupation. Resources. Power. Status.

That Place did not/would never want to be seen as a nation that backed down from a fight. And if This Place continued battling their presence, a fight is exactly what they would get.

My father threw a fit when I showed him "The Year it Began." "Where did you get this fucking ridiculous propaganda?" Never a good way to start a conversation.

I tried to explain the context to him. That I was asking for his response as part of an initiative that a friend—I hope it's not too soon to call you that, I know it's only been a few months—in This Place is designing. That the texts have been written by a group of young people in This Place who want to show That Placers their history, as they have learned it. That it is a student-led effort to explore how we approach alternative versions of the histories that we have been raised to consider as 'truth.'

"I knew we should have never let you go there," was Dad's witty comeback to my attempt at contextualisation. My parents have never had much of a say in where I go or what I do, but it was interesting to see the paternal rage and vitriol and nationalism ooze out of him… I never remembered my father as having such strong views about This Place. I guess I was wrong.

The phrase that really set him off in the extract was the reference to "more-evolved governments." That phrasing catalysed an entire diatribe about how the text was probably influenced by agents from the Other Place. "We saved them," he said. That Place saved This Place from a terrible fate. And that's that.

Have you had other responses like this? There must be quite a number of responses that express similar ideologies—responses fuelled by unquestioned patriotism rather than a desire for an informed opinion? Are you seeing a trend in the That Place demographic that tends to respond in such a way? Does it tend to be people from the socioeconomic elite who are less open to changing their minds because they already consider themselves to be 'educated enough'? Are women more likely to be receptive to new ways of looking at history, since we're conditioned to be/pretend to be malleable to different opinions? Are younger people more resistant to changing their views as compared to an older generation that might have had to face the brunt of suffering from ongoing eruptions of violence?

I know I'm just one of the many data gatherers that you're working with, but if you have the time—and if you think I can be trusted with this information—I would love to learn more about your findings. I understand that you might not want to, of course. These are risky times, and I don't want you to be worried about my intentions. I am well aware that some of your colleagues think of me as an agent looking to get dissenting citizens on both sides into trouble with the government. So, yes, I completely understand if you'd rather not share your findings with me. I'm happy to wait till you think I can be trusted.

2:45:30 PM

◆ How did they sound?

■ Who?

◆ Her fathers.

■ Fine. Tired. Stressed.

◆ No one wants to deal with this on their daughter's wedding day.

■ They were expecting us hours ago. The ceremony would have been finished by now. We'd be well into the after-party.

\ \ \ \ \ \ \

◆ I hope they let her get changed into something comfortable at least . . .

■ What?

◆ All of this paraphernalia is heavy! I hope she can change out of it till we know when we can get there.

> . . . the bride's clothing situation is probably
> the last thing that they are thinking about.
> And even if they do, the last thing she's likely
> to want is to take off all of the . . . what did

you call it? Paraphernalia? . . . She's from
here . . . she knows that things can change
in the blink of an eye . . . She's more likely
to want to wait, till she's absolutely sure that
things are going to be postponed before making any attempt to . . . you know . . . do something like that. ▪

◆ Do something like what? Change her clothes?

It probably took hours for her to put it all on in the first
place. She won't want to do that again. Unless there's a
delay of . . . I don't know . . . more than a few hours. ▪

◆ So, she'll just sit in all that . . .

Probably. ▪

◆ For how many hours?

There's no formula for this stuff. ▪

◆ If you had to guess?

I don't know. ▪

◆ Ballpark?

Why does it matter to you so much? ▪

◆ You have no idea how uncomfortable it is to wear all this.

So, you take it off! She'll be fine. ▪

◆ You don't know that.

I do know that. Do you know how many curfews she has experienced? She knows the drill.
This is part of her normal. She will adapt. ▪

◆ This is her wedding! This curfew is not like any of the others, however many there might have been.

It's always someone's wedding. ▪

◆ Why are you being like this?

Like what? ▪

◆ I'm just trying to understand . . . You don't have to be a jerk about it.
I'm going to change.

She hated it when he got like this. When he was antagonistic for
the sake of being antagonistic. She just wanted to understand. Even
though she knew that she wouldn't, and couldn't, ever fully understand This Place, the attempt was important to her. The attempt to
understand all of the things about This Place that were indecipher-
able. The attempt to be a better ally—to constantly acknowledge her
own ignorance by asking more questions. This attempt to understand
was important to her on a micro, individual level, sure. But it was also
important to her on a larger scale, as a political statement.

From her limited interactions with This Place and its people, she
had come to believe that a fundamental cause for the ongoing con-

flict was the unwillingness of That Placers to try and understand This Place. Therefore, as part of this political principle that she had come to think of as being invaluable, she wanted more people from That Place to try and imagine the conditions in This Place. Through this imagination and empathy, she hoped that people from That Place would be less likely to see This Place and its conflicts in black-and-white terms. Through this imagination and empathy, she hoped that people from That Place would be better positioned to understand the extent of the violations their government was imposing in This Place, in their name.

She wanted more people from That Place to try and understand This Place. Such attempts, she thinks, are the only possible way in which connections might be catalysed between the peoples of these regions. People from That Place need to understand. They need to make the effort to understand.

He knew that was important to her too. He knew because she had told him. Many times. That's why she always asked so many questions. Why it was so pivotal for her to try and understand more. He knew that. She had told him.

Fucker. Why did he have to talk to her like that? In that patronising tone. Fucking men . . . War zone or not, they're all the same when it comes to thinking that they know better.

She stopped in the midst of that thought, in the midst of changing out of the wedding paraphernalia, to take a deep breath and prevent her mind from going down the rabbit hole of generalisations. Neither This Place nor That needed more of those. Generalisations.

Breathe in.
Breathe out.
Breathe in.
Breathe out.

As she exhaled for the fifth time, she realised that the door to her changing room was slightly ajar. And that he could probably see her silhouette as she got out of the wedding paraphernalia. The wedding paraphernalia that she was really uncomfortable in. A discomfort that was the only reason guiding her attempt to sympathise with the bride's clothing. Clearly that was a mistake.

Fucking men w—No.

Breathe in.
Breathe out.
Breathe in.
Breathe out.
Breathe in.

This time, on her last exhalation, she reached out to close the door, to make sure that he couldn't see her silhouette. But as her hand reached the handle, she realised that she didn't want to close the door. She wanted him to see her form. Maybe that would teach him not to take her for granted. If he got a glimpse of what he was missing out on.

This thought lasted for a split second because she realised that as soon as she thought, *Let him see what he's missing out on*, she was considering using her body as bait to make a man feel guilty about something he had said or done. She had to stop that thought immediately. That was another rabbit hole that nobody needed to go down.

Breathe in.
Breathe out.
Breathe in.
Breathe out.
Breathe in.

She hated it when he got like this. When he was antagonistic just for the sake of being antagonistic. Mostly because he was rarely ever antagonistic. He was one of the most patient and amenable people that she had ever met. And, usually, no matter how inane the question that she asked him, he would do his best to respond to her.

This had been true from the first time they'd met, at a friend's house, during her second year of visiting This Place. From the moment they'd met, despite his initial reticence at liaising with someone who worked with soldiers, he gave her a chance—not many This Placers would give average That Placers a chance, let alone persons like her who worked with the armed forces. Over the years, he had become her first point of contact anytime she had a question. He had indulged her curfew simulation despite his own doubts about it. He had given her interesting insights to reflect upon for her Curriculum. Over the last five years, he had become her sounding board. Her partner-in-idealism.

And she had become his.

It was this underlying, built-over-the-years partnership that made his occasional snappy comments hard for her to understand. Because these comments made her feel like she had crossed a line she didn't know existed. Because the particular tone of voice that he used in such comments communicated to her that he was in bad shape—in his head, in his heart—and that she could do nothing to help him because she didn't understand. She couldn't understand. She'd never understand.

However hard she tried, there would always be some things that escaped her. Because she was not from This Place.

Sometimes, she thought they'd come to see each other as being beyond their This Place/That Place identities. No, that's not true. Sometimes, she believed that they—more than most — were likelier to see each other as being beyond their nationalities. Which is why it still surprised her when the occupation would intrude, and she would feel him moving away from her. She knew he felt it too. Even if they were sitting right next to each other, when something about the differences in their lived experiences emerged, she'd feel him slipping away. Spaces kept coming between them.

She left that door just ever so slightly ajar until she was ready to step back out again. Relieved from the heavy and uncomfortable trappings that she was carrying on her body, like deadweight. If her paraphernalia was this heavy, imagine the poor bride.

She left the door slightly ajar because . . . well, she wanted to remind him of that thing between them. The thing that neither of them could/wanted to name. The thing that he needed to remember, so that he knew he couldn't take her for granted.

Out of her heavy clothes, she still took a few minutes to compose herself.

Breathe in.
Breathe out.
Breathe in.
Breathe out.
Breathe in.
Breathe out.

She needed to compose herself before going back out there. Because when she was not composed, she had the tendency to say things that she regretted.

Didn't he realise how difficult he was being? Did he need her to tell him that he was being a jerk? Couldn't he appreciate the effort she made? Wasn't that one of the things that connected them in the first place?

I've never met someone like you before. Especially from That Place. Someone who so earnestly wants to understand my life and the lives of others in This Place. Someone who is so intrigued by the most banal details. I love that everything is significant to you. That nothing is unimportant.

He'd said that. Those words. Exactly.

Fucker.
She imagined him watching her through the sliver of space in that door. Watching the curve of her waist. Feeling that familiar pull that had become a regular occurrence for them both.

You better realise that I'm special to you, motherfucker. And stop being an ass.

3:06 PM

\ \ \ \ \ \ \

I'm sorry I was a bit . . . snappy. ▪

◆ Mmmhmmm.

We're okay, right? ▪

◆ I'm still a little bit annoyed with you, but we'll be fine.

▪ I know you're trying to understand. I just . . . look . . . Sometimes, it's just hard to explain things when . . . when we're in the middle of something that feels like it's going to be catastrophic . . . The removal of the Guarantee, it feels catastrophic. It's going to unleash something we've never seen before because it's never happened before. Not like this . . . It terrifies me.

\ \ \ \ \ \ \

- ◆ I'm sorry.

- ▪ You have nothing to apologize for. I just . . . I'm going to be snappy today. I'll try not to be. I love answering your questions and thinking about how to articulate . . . you know . . . these things that I usually take for granted. It's just . . . on days like today, the nerves get the better of me whether I want them to or not. So, be patient with me, okay?

- ◆ As long as you'll be patient with me.

- ▪ Always.

\ \ \ \ \ \ \

- ▪ To answer your question, the wedding protocols here—especially for brides—are incredibly tedious. So, she has probably been in ceremonies and rituals since sunrise. And a lot of those things, for the lack of a better word, that they do in those ceremonies involve blessing the different items that she's wearing . . . you know? The jewellery. The clothes. The little pieces that adorn her hair. All of it is blessed during those early wedding rituals. So, it's not as simple as her just changing out of the clothes . . . because changing would mean starting all those rituals from scratch and that—It's just a lot. Right now, she's probably hoping the curfew will pass.

- ◆ I didn't know that . . . about the rituals, I mean. Well, I knew that there were lots of ceremonies, but I didn't know that they had to do with . . . you know . . . paraphernalia . . .

- ■ I'm sure she's devastated. I'm sure her dads are devastated too. Our parents have lived through so many more of these than us, but even they probably didn't think that something as momentous as this would happen on their children's wedding day.

\ \ \ \ \ \ \

- ■ That's the wonder of it . . . they actually sounded surprised on the phone. After everything they've been through, after all the curfews and cancelled weddings that they've seen, both sets of parents sounded surprised that they had to tell us to hold off till things calmed down.

- ◆ It is a surprise, isn't it?

- ■ I guess . . .

- ◆ Isn't it?

- ■ It should be.

- ◆ But you're not surprised.

- I don't know. Maybe I am. Surprised that it happened today as opposed to tomorrow. Surprised that it occurred at this moment in time, rather than at another one. The specific timing of all of this is surprising. But . . . but am I surprised that this happened? In general? Here? In This Place? No. I can't say that I am. This is what they do. This is what it does. This is what occupation looks like. Where's the surprise in that, you know? Today, it happened during the wedding of someone we know. Yesterday, it was during the naming ceremony of the neighbour's child. The day before that, during someone's funeral. Before that, during a birthday party. Tomorrow, while a mother gives birth. The particular moment in which the curfew happens is always surprising. Not the occurrence, though. Not the action.

- I've never heard you use that word before.

- Surprise?

- Occupation.

                                                          Oh. -

- I've just . . . I've never heard you use that word before.

                    It's not a word that I like to use . . . you know . . .
                                        in front of you. -

- Right.

                    It's not a word that I like to use in front of anyone
                    from That Place, like you, who is trying to un-
                    derstand . . . to make sense of it all. I don't use

that word in front of people like you. I find that
it's—It can be alienating. ■

◆ It's a strong word.

Right. ■

◆ It's not untrue.

I really don't want to alienate you. ■

◆ I know.

■ That's literally the opposite of what I want. All I meant—

◆ I know what you meant.

■ I meant—

◆ No, really. I get it. I'm not taking it personally.

■ Yes. Good.

\ \ \ \ \ \ \

- Because I know you're not them.

- I'm not them.

- No. You're just—

- I'm just from there.

- Yes.

- From the land of the occupiers.

- I should have—

- It's fine. I told you. It's fine. I'm fine. We're fine. We don't have to talk about this anymore.

- I can see that I've upset you.

- No, no it's not you. It's just . . . this. All of this. You're right. It is an occupation. And I'm from That Place. That Place of occupiers. I . . . I don't know how to sit with that knowledge.

- Being from the land of occupiers, and being one yourself, are two different things.

- But . . . it's a fine line, isn't it? Is the occupier only the government that allows this to happen, and the person who is on the streets, holding the gun to carry out that government's orders? Or is it also the person from That Place who knows what is happening and doesn't do anything about it? Is it also the person from That Place who does something, knowing that it won't be enough to dismantle the occupation? Is it also the person from That Place who chooses not to know what is being done in their name? Is it also the person who continues to pay taxes even after knowing what is being done in their name? What about the person who turns a blind eye to what's happening because they can't be bothered? Or because they are so consumed by their own daily occupations that they cannot see past the murk? Or—

Stop. Please. ■

◆ I'm not as upset as listing those things made me sound.

Who said anything about being up— ■

◆ You asked me to stop.

■ Not becau—I asked you to stop because that list could go on forever. And I see the point you're trying to make. The categories are complex, perhaps, but the category of "occupier," it . . . it doesn't apply to all those people. It applies to the government. To the people who enact the government's word. To the people who ask the government to continue that work in This Place. But it doesn't apply to those who are—

◆ Complicit?

■ Well, there are different layers to complicity and different, different degrees of . . . of . . .

◆ There are degrees of separation, yes. But the centre of the circle? That's the same. It's the occupation. Wherever you lie, it's in relation to that centre. So . . . ergo . . . Somehow, when you call this an occupation, am I not one of the occupiers?

■ Okay. Let's say for argument's sake. Only for the sake of argument that I agree with your logic. I'm not saying that I do, but for argument's sake, let's say that I do. How does that help anything? How does making you part of a catchall category help any of us?

◆ It helps just like other labels and categories do. It helps create a situational framework. Where we are all clear about where we stand.

■ Okay . . . and in this moment. In this situation. Where two people from This Place and That Place are waiting for a wedding to get back on track, how does that situational framework help?

◆ It helps remind me that . . . that . . . we . . . us . . . this . . . I don't know.

They sat in more silence. Like they always did when the outside came in. When their camaraderie and friendship-with-undercurrents and their conversations and their interactions were invaded by the reality of the occupation. When they were forced to come to terms with being from opposing sides of a war. When they were forced to recognise the imbalances of power that came from nationhood and subjecthood. When the two of them had to reckon with the reality of what it would mean to explore their undercurrents, as they found themselves wanting to. More and more every day.

When words like 'occupation' emerged, they had to really look at the chasms that separated them. And consider the possibility that nothing—no effort, no conversation, no attempt, no goal of understanding—might ever be enough to bring them together in the way that they wanted to be brought together. In the way that, if they were being really honest with themselves, they fantasised about being together. When words like 'occupation' were not mentioned, they could lull themselves into a false sense of security. A sense of hope. A sense that maybe another world was possible. That maybe, if more people from This Place and That Place really tried to talk to each other, if more people from This Place and That Place really tried to understand each other, the occupation would dissipate into insignificance. When words like 'occupation' went unmentioned, they could convince themselves that it didn't matter that they came from opposing sides. They could allow the lack of naming to create the illusion of a relationship between equal peers. They could do all this. Until words like 'occupation' emerged in conversation. Intentionally. Flippantly. In whatever way.

When words like 'occupation' emerged in conversation, reality always hit home. The reality that whatever the undercurrents between them, whatever connection they shared, whatever attempt they made to understand, whatever hope they had for their micro status quo as symbolising vis-à-vis a macro shift . . . When words like 'occupation' emerged in conversation, they were reminded that nothing could change, until the occupation ended.

Nothing between them could change, until the occupation ended.

Talk about impossible stakes.

WHERE IT BEGAN

My mother insists that I document her responses within the sections themselves. She wants to "talk to him, without talking to him," apparently. So, here are her thoughts, included inline within the text that provoked them.

I have to warn you in advance: my mother thinks in unpredictable ways. She draws connections between things that most wouldn't see. I suppose that's where I get it from!

Anyway, here you go. I hope this is useful.

XXXX: THE YEAR THE FIRST THING HAPPENED

And then the First Uprising happened. When various leaders from across revolutionary groups got together in the Square and went on a hunger strike, demanding a political solution to This Place's conflicts. They all sat down in the main square, holding hands, chanting slogans that asked That Place to leave, inviting guest speakers to address the gathering crowds about ways in which they needed to come together to decide their fate. And to fight for the kind of future that they wanted. It was a completely peaceful event. Until the soldiers came at them. With sticks. And guns. And unleashed utter mayhem on revolutionaries who were simply attempting to get together and demand the kind of future that they wanted for This Place. And once the army fired the first shot, there was no way the leaders could tell others in their midst to just stand back and allow themselves to be razed to the ground. When attacked, they attacked back. But the first shot, they fired it. The soldiers. From That Place. There were almost one hundred martyrs who lost their lives that day. More who were arrested for simply being in the wrong place at the wrong time. A handful who simply disappeared that day, never to be seen again.

The first thing my mom wants you to know is that her father's brother's son (my cousin?) was stationed in This Place during the time this happened. She wants you to know this just in case I have obfuscated the truth and not told you about my familial connection to the armed forces. She's standing over my shoulder as I write this, to ensure that it is written.

She says that you need to know this context because everything that she has heard, everything that she knows about the Year the First Thing Happened, is defined by her uncle relaying information from his son on the ground. She wants you to know that her uncle talked about the ways in which the soldiers were targeted by the terrorists. She wants you to know that her nephew sustained a head injury that day, from a stone that was hurled at him by the protesters who initially said that they were going to manifest peacefully.

She also says (yes, she's still standing behind me) that because of this 'firsthand' knowledge of what happened there that year (no, she does not like the fact that I used quotation marks around 'firsthand'), she cannot help but look at this text with some scepticism. Her nephew has an injury which proves, to her, that he is telling the truth. I honestly do not get that jump in her logic, but that's what she says.

Although it was a failure in terms of the goals for the uprising—to foster political solutions to the issue at hand—this event marked a turning point in the spirit of This Place. A turning point after which the fallen heroes of This Place were spoken about extensively to the younger generations as role models. For many of the young This Placers, the First Uprising marked a momentous turn in the spirit of This Place. A turn that might never have taken place if the soldiers hadn't fired that first shot. If the soldiers had not fired that shot, maybe this event would simply have been forgotten in the passages of history as a failed protest. As a failed effort by the leaders of This Place. Instead, by firing that shot, by making martyrs of the leaders, That Place's soldiers had actually helped highlight the potential of protest. They had actually helped the event be seen as an uprising, rather than a ragtag group of people getting together to talk about the future of their homeland.

My mom wants you to know that her nephew suffered. That he was in the intensive care unit for three weeks. That they were worried about paralysis. That it was a miracle when he came out of that event as unscathed as he did.

She wants me to tell you that she appreciates how you're teaching me the ropes of This Place, and that she's happy I have someone I can call a friend. But, that being said, she doesn't believe this account of the Year the First Thing Happened. She can't, she says, because it would dishonour what happened to her nephew.

As a result of the First Uprising, citizens of This Place were given visible proof of the violence of the oppressor. The oppressor who would take down anyone who stood in their way. As a result of the First Uprising, leaders who made it out of that event alive became local heroes who could then inspire young people in their neighbourhoods. As a result of the First Uprising, This Place found its way onto the news outlets of That Place and the world beyond. This Place couldn't be ignored any more. The First Uprising had put their resistance on the map. There was no turning back now.

She liked watching him like this. Unguarded. Quiet. Doing his own thing. It was a complex form of anthropological research. Voyeurism.

> Left. Gobble. Snake grows longer. Up. Up. Gobble. Snake grows longer. Shift Direction. Weave. Hit the wall. Snake explodes. Restart game. Up. Wait. Clear the wall. Left. Clear the Wall. Right. Wait. Gobble. Snake grows longer. Wait. Wait. Weave. Hit the wall. Snake explodes. Restart game. Dodge. Gobble. Snake grows longer. Up. Right. Gobble. Snake grows longer. Keep going. Down. Wait. Clear the Wall. Gobble. Snake grows longer. Left. Clear the Wall. Down. Gobble.

He looked beautiful in this light.

> Hit the wall. Snake explodes. Restart game. Down. Right. Right. Dodge. Left. Up. Up. Clear the Wall. Clear the Wall. Wait. Left. Up. Up. Left. Clear the Wall. Wait. Gobble. Snake grows longer. Wait. Up. Left. Gobble. Snake grows longer. Wait. Gobble. Snake grows longer. Gobble. Snake grows longer. Hit the wall. Snake explodes. Restart game. Squiggle. Down. Wait. Up. Gobble. Snake grows longer. Right. Left. Weave. Hit the wall. Snake explodes. Restart game.

She loved watching him twirl the lock of hair that kept falling onto his forehead.

Wait. Right. Gobble. Snake grows longer. Up. Gobble. Snake grows longer. Gobble. Snake grows longer. Keep going. Right. Wait. Shift direction. Up. Hit the wall. Snake explodes. Restart game. Wait. Dodge. Up. Left. Gobble. Snake grows longer. Up. Gobble. Snake grows longer. Clear the Wall. Gobble.

The lines under his eyes. The rugged beauty of exhausted idealism.

Down. Up. Clear the wall. Clear the wall. Squiggle. Weave. Down. Left. Gobble. Snake grows longer. Gobble. Down. Clear the wall. Weave. Gobble. Snake grows longer. Hit the wall. Snake explodes. Restart game. Straight. Up. Hit the wall. Snake explodes. Restart game.

She couldn't look away sometimes. Many times, actually. More times, every time.

She needed to stop staring at him.

Just close your eyes. That'll stop you from staring.

- How long have I been asleep?

- Not that long. You can go back to sleep if you like.

- Mmmm . . .

\ \ \ \ \ \ \

◆ Is the internet back up?

▪ No.

◆ I thought I saw you on your phone.

▪ Just looking through old photos.

◆ Mmm . . .

▪ Good nap?

◆ Mmmhmm . . . What have you been doing?

▪ Passing time.

He wished that her shawl would slip a little bit, so that he could see that collarbone that he was so enchanted with. It didn't, of course. *Nothing you want to happen ever does.* Watching her there, eyes closed, resting, he couldn't help but try to put himself in her shoes. *What was she thinking about? What was she dreaming about? How could she sleep in a time like this?*

The windy roads had taken it out of her, she'd told him. The nausea that even the anti-nausea pills couldn't seem to contain. She'd recounted the exhausting experience of taking the bus to This Place, with her head sticking out the window because fresh air was the only thing that seemed to help the imminent retching subside. She usually flew to This Place and he knew that made her feel a little bit . . . pretentious. Like she was too good to take the bus or the train like most people who travelled between That Place and This Place. That's why she'd come by road this time. Because, the last time she was here, he had told her that traveling by bus or train was the only way to truly see the way in which the landscape shifted—so sharply—when one crossed over from That Place into This one. Like even the lines of the land were saying, "Hey, you're entering different territory."

When he went to pick her up at the bus station, she'd told him that she now understood what he had meant. That even through the churning in her stomach, even through the bile in her throat, she could see that dramatic shift in the shapes and lines and curves of the land. From the flatness of desert to the ruggedness of peaks. Even through the nausea, she could see that. Appreciate that. Admire that. Some things are worth throwing up for.

She looked beautiful with the sleep laying heavily on her lids. Don't be a creep and look at her as she's waking up. You're going to make her uncomfortable.

His eyes were hurting from looking at that damn screen for so long. That always seemed to happen during curfewed days. He could feel them watering from the strain. Maybe he should do some of those eye exercises that someone had told him about.

Close your eyes.
Look to the right.
Hold for ten seconds.
One.
Two.
Three.
Four.
Five.
Six.
Seven.
Eight.
Nine.
Ten.
Look to the left.
Hold for ten seconds.
One.
Two.
Three.

Four.
Five.
Six.
Seven.
Eight.
Nine.
Ten.

Repeat this a few times.

Keeping the eyes closed,
Look around.
Move eyeballs in a circle, clockwise.
One.
Two.
Three.
Four.
Five.
Six.
Seven.
Eight.
Nine.
Ten.

Keeping the eyes closed,
Look around.
Move eyeballs in a circle,
      anticlockwise.
One.
Two.
Three.
Four.

Five.
Six.
Seven.
Eight.
Nine.
Ten.

Repeat this a few times, in both directions.

Keeping the eyes closed,
Look up for ten seconds.
One.
T—.

◆ Want to watch something? Or are we still not at The Gaze intimacy level yet?

▪ Wh—I—yo—fuck off. What do you have?

◆ A few different options. Here, look through it.

▪ We better not use up all the battery though. Power could go off later.

◆ I think it's full. We should be fine to use it for one movie.

\ \ \ \ \ \ \

- Wow. You have a lot of shit on this thing!

♦ Your brother was the one who gave me most of those movies.

- Any one of these that you haven't watched?

♦ I haven't watched most of them. I got an entirely new stash from him after I used up all the old ones during the curfew simulation.

- I've seen most of these . . . let me see . . .

\ \ \ \ \ \ \

- Here, this one. I've been meaning to rewatch it for a while anyway. That ok with you?

♦ The Shakespeare adaptation? Really?

- I knew you'd roll your eyes! Look, it's a really well researched representation of the Golden Age. You're the one who keeps saying you want to learn as much as possible about how things are here!

♦ I do say that, don't I. Fuck me.

- Besides, a group of us have been talking about using this movie in an event sometime soon . . . as a counterpoint to other mainstream movies . . . to really dig into the role of That Place's film industry in perpetuating particular problematic representations of This Place.

♦ Tell the film industry to stop looking toward old, white, male writers as the gold standard of everything literary, and to take risks on new voices. That'd be a good start.

- I'll pick another movie.

◆ No. Stop. It's fine. I'm just being an ass.

- I promise this movie has plenty of material for you to ask a gazillion questions about.

◆ Very funny.

- You want to move over here or should I—

◆ Come here.

- Move over a little bit, then.

◆ Good?

- Good. Let me just hook the speaker up. There we go.

◆ Comfy?

- Yeah. You?

◆ Yeah.

Set in the Golden Age of Revolution, a Doctor based in the capital of This Place agrees to perform an appendectomy on the Leader of a revolutionary group. In order to avoid detection by That Place authorities, who would want him to turn in the Leader, the Doctor performs the surgery at his house, much to the chagrin of his Wife, who is upset at the medical professional's unilateral decision to place their entire household at risk.

*Am I sitting too close to him? I think I'm
sitting too close to him.
Move over just a little bit this way.
Perfect.*

> *Why is she moving away? I wonder if I sat
> too close. I should change positions so that
> she doesn't feel uncomfortable. Perfect.*

Why is he moving aw—fuck it. Stop.

> *Focus on the movie. You've been wanting
> to rewatch this forever.*

Focus on the movie.

                    Focus on the movie.

Focus on the movie.

                    Focus on the movie.

Focus on the movie.

                    Focus on the movie.

Focus on the movie.

                    Focus on the movie.

Focus on the movie.

                    Focus on the movie.

> The following day, That Place's authorities somehow discover that the Doctor has a Leader in his home and organise a military raid, unannounced. The Doctor is accused of treason, for harbouring the Leader, and when the Leader attempts to make an escape, a shoot-out ensues. As a consequence of this—

◆ Wait, it's not illegal for him to provide medical treatment to a Leader. So, what are the grounds for the soldiers just coming into his house like that, without an arrest warrant?

▪ First, they don't need cause to come into people's homes. Second, the movie is set during the Golden Age, no?

◆ So?

▪ During the Golden Age, no one was allowed to let a Leader into their homes without calling the authorities. So technically, within that particular ... what do you call it? Context of the ... I can't find words right now apparently. Let me try again. Ok. So. Within the timeframe that they're focusing ...

■ Within the timeframe that they're focusing on in the film, they're right. It would have been completely illegal for a Doctor to let a Leader into their home without informing authorities.

♦ I didn't know that ...

■ That's how they used to identify what they called the 'collaborators.' People who would have leaders and fighters sheltered in their homes, but who wouldn't call the authorities immediately. In the eyes of That Place, if you didn't call the authorities when these people came into your home, you probably were sympathisers of some kind and deserved to be punished for your actions.

♦ That sounds overly simplistic.

■ Of course, it is. There are many reasons why people wouldn't or couldn't call the authorities if fighters or revolutionaries came into their homes ... some were sympathisers, sure. But there were plenty of other reasons.

♦ They could have been threatened by the fighters, right?

■ Of course. And sometimes, people couldn't call simply because the phone lines weren't working. You couldn't tell the authorities because you were on lockdown, couldn't leave your home, and the phones didn't work . . . I told you this movie would teach you things!

The Leader is killed and the Doctor is taken away by That Place's authorities and placed under arrest. And upon his being taken away that day, the Doctor is never seen or heard from again. Despite multiple efforts by his Wife to contact the relevant authorities for information about where Doctor is being held, the family is given no updates as to his whereabouts. The Doctor has, for all intents and purposes, disappeared.

A few months later, worried that the Doctor hasn't returned home, his Son returns from University—an institution in That Place—to seek answers about his father's disappearance. He has already checked all the detention centres in That Place that are known to incarcerate collaborators from This Place. Now, his only option is to search the detention centres in This Place. (It should go without saying that if someone cannot be located in any of the detention centres in This or That Place, they'll probably never be seen or heard from again.)

Upon his return home, the Son is shocked to discover that his mother (Wife) seems to be pursuing a relationship with the Doctor's brother (Uncle).

WHERE IT BEGAN

Here's the text for the next phase. I'm really looking forward to seeing who you decide to speak with about it. Are you thinking of venturing outside family? Not that I have a preference of course. This is your dataset. You get to decide.

You're right. I have been stepping back and allowing you to share aspects of yourself without volunteering anything about my own life. A part of me wants to say that I'm wary because of past experience ... that I've met too many people from That Place who say they want to get to know me, only to then use my experiences as badges of honour. To tell their friends that they know people who live in This Place: this land of occupations and war and bloodshed.

If I'm being honest though, that's not really the reason. Not that there haven't been those leeches, there certainly have. But I know each person is different and I know when to trust my instincts about people.

Honestly, I think it's just been easier to let you take the lead on sharing. It's a hard thing for me. To share. To confide. It seems to come naturally to some, you know? Some people ... my brother is one of them ... he's really good at sharing parts of himself even with people he's just met. And he does this openly. Without expectation. Without fear. He shares himself because it's the only way he knows how to be. Whereas I tend to take more time. It takes time for me to reveal myself ...

So, I'm going to need you to help me out. Take the lead. At least in the beginning. Ask me questions. Tell me what you want to know. Help me draw myself out.

You up for that?

XXXX–XXXX: THE GOLDEN AGE OF REVOLUTION

The First Uprising led to a Golden Age of Revolution. Of course, That Place calls it the period of The Wave.

The Wave of Terrorism.

The Golden Age of Revolution was a rich and vibrant time. A decade during which artists and activists and cultural workers and public intellectuals and academics and students and mothers and lawyers and daughters spoke eloquently and creatively about their cause. About their fight. The Golden Age of Revolution was a time that gave birth to 'fighters': people, young and old, who were not affiliated with any of the revolutionary groups, but who still took to the streets. Fighters who took to the streets with their ideas and their stones and their picket signs and their poetry to ensure that their fights—their individual, micro fights—would become part of a complex revolutionary fabric. The Golden Age of Revolution was a time of hope. It was a decade during which every citizen of This Place, in one way or the other, became part of the revolution.

For some, this meant becoming a fighter. For some, this meant sheltering a fighter. For some, this meant making sure that fighters-in-hiding would have access to food and medical supplies. For some, this meant engaging in deep and pious prayer to help ensure freedom would come. For some, this meant finding more ways to connect with people in the Other Place, because there was more solace to be found there. For some, this meant using the resources of That Place, like the educational institutions and resources, and then bringing all their knowledge and skills back to This Place. For some, this meant creating art. Creating beautiful works of literature and sculpture and film and drama to bear witness to their time.

The Golden Age was golden for that reason. It was a time during which every citizen of This Place found their own way to manifest their particular views. It was a time of the triumph of the individual spirit. A testament to the sheer force and beauty of a mosaic of voices that together, composed the voice of a nation. In This Place, the Golden Age of Revolution was spoken about, and taught to those who hadn't lived it, as a spectacular age of resistance. An age that culminated with the release of the Golden Manifesto that would come to define the region for years to come. In classrooms and homes and restaurants in This Place, the Manifesto became a revered document. And even when That Place's government ignored its calls for action, even when nothing seemed to be happening at a macro level, the Golden Manifesto represented hope for the people of This Place.

Yes, I'm up for that. Asking questions has never been a problem for me. Here's hoping you don't get sick of my questions. Or me!

So, for this text, I decided to venture one degree outside my immediate family and talk to a cousin who is like a sister to me. And, as I expected, her responses are closely aligned to mine.

She critiqued the fact that our history books have never included anything about the fertile ground the Golden Age represented for This Placers. She recounted the ways in which Terrorism was highlighted in everything that she has seen or heard or read about that time.

She also expressed a keen desire to replicate your initiative on this side of the border. Where a group of young people on our end would create texts that showcase how history is taught to us, and then send them over to you, to get responses from This Placers.

I told her that I wasn't sure this is a both-sides-of-the-border kind of thing (please correct me if I'm wrong). It seems to me that people in This Place are already well aware of how we learn history. It's our side that needs more information, more nuance.

Funny thing, that. The powerless always seem to know more about the powerful than the powerful know about them...

So, here's a question to draw you out: last time we met, you briefly mentioned that you had started writing a "Guide to Curfew Timepass," or something like that. Tell me more?

♦ You studied there for a few years, right? The same school that the Son guy went to?

■ Well, yeah. But many years later. The reference they make about the University accommodation in that scene, that was not true by the time I went there. When I went, students from This Place and That Place had mixed dorms.

♦ Did you like being there? At the University?

■ At the University, sure. I made some great friends. I took some great classes, had fantastic professors and all of that. At the time, it was also the only University in this region that was offering a major like Protest Psychology. So yeah, many good things . . . But I also didn't have much of a choice in going there, given what I wanted to study.

♦ Life outside the University wasn't something you enjoyed? I don't think we've ever talked about that.

■ That's a tough one because I don't know how much was . . . you know, I felt some discrimination, certainly. Especially from the cops. That year the rule was that students from This Place had to report to the police station once every two weeks so that they could make sure we were there doing what we were supposed to be doing and not, I don't know, planning an attack or whatever it is they think we do. Anyway, I'd always get shit from the cops during these check-ins because of the Protest Psychology major . . . obviously. Just the usual crap: "Why are you studying this subject?" "Are you planning to become a terrorist" et cetera, et cetera. It sucked but . . . it was also to be expected. Outside of that sort of 'explicit' discrimination, if you will, I don't know, I felt like I was never at home there. Never welcome. Never wanted. But I also don't know how much of that feeling was actually because particular things were said and done or how much of it was because I didn't, you know, allow That Place to grow on me. Does that make sense?

◆ Yeah. Absolutely. It was your first time away from home, no?

▪ Yeah. First time. And it was That Place. So, it came with a lot of baggage . . . The only way I could justify it to myself was that I was there to learn what I could, get the hell out, and come back home.

◆ Were your folks okay with you going there to study?

▪ Yeah. It was hard but they know that here—I mean you know how it is. Between the shutdowns and everything, I would have been able to go to University for maybe three months out of an entire academic year—if I was lucky. And the administrators would have kept pushing me through because they don't want to hold students back and—Wait, you need to watch this part. It's beautifully shot.

> Unable to understand Wife's behaviour, Son begins searching for Doctor across detention centres in This Place, with the help of his childhood Sweetheart (who is now a badass fighter of some kind). Sweetheart soon finds an Informant who tells Son that she (the Informant) had been imprisoned with Doctor, in a detention centre that was hidden in the rugged mountains of This Place.

5:22:50 PM

◆ That is some beautiful cinematography, right?

▪ Gorgeous work.

Of course, he asks me to pay attention to a romantic reunion between two lovers. Cinematography, my ass. This is totally a strategy to change the conversation and the mood. I know he wants to have that conversation and he's just trying to get me in the mood for it. Well, if he wants to have the conversation, he needs to just come out and say it! Directly. Fuck, you're spinning out. He asked you to look at cinematography. Maybe that's all he's asking you to do, without any hidden agenda.

> *Focus on the movie.*
> *Focus on the movie.*
> *Focus on the movie.*
> *Focus on the movie.*
> *Focus on the movie.*

> *Look at that gorgeousness. Perfect backdrop for a nostalgic flash-back to the couple's first kiss. I hope the romance is not lost on him . . .*
> *Of course, it's not. It's probably why he chose this movie to begin with. Research for an event, my arse. He just wanted me to watch this scene to set the stage f—Okay. Stop. You're spinning out again. Why are you obsessing about the conversation? You know that it is not going to end well. You don't want it to happen. Idiot.*

Still it would be nice if he moved a little closer again. Maybe we could hold hands. Holding hands is fine, right? Friends hold hands all the time. It wouldn't have to mea—Stop it. No holding hands. That would mean something. You know it would mean something. And then you'll have to talk about things. Stop it. Just focus on the fucking cinematography.

Focus on the movie.
Focus on the movie.
Focus on the movie.
Maybe I could just rest my head on his shou—

Focus on the movie.
Focus on the movie.

Fuck, he smells good.

Informant tells Son about her conversations with Doctor in the detention centre, a facility in which they had been held and tortured for interminable weeks. Informant reveals that Doctor suspected Uncle, his own brother, as having been the person to send That Place authorities to his home. Now, how did Uncle even know that Doctor was harbouring a Leader in his home? Doctor didn't seem to know. Informant tells Son that Doctor wanted Son to avenge the injustice meted out to him. This desire for vengeance was what the Doctor shared with Informant before finally acquiescing to the wounds that had been inflicted on him by That Place's authorities. Hearing this, Son suffers a—

♦ What the fuck was that?

- Stay here, yeah? I'll be right back.

◆ Where are you—

- Just give me a second. I'm going to go downstairs and see what's happening. Don't worry, it's probably nothing. Keep watching.

She pauses the movie and looks out the window. Nothing. She hears their voices downstairs. Unintelligible sounds. What if she went closer to the door? What about the balcony? No. Still just unintelligible sounds. No words that she understands, anyway.

It's ok. You know what they're talking about. They are just trying to figure out what the sound was.

That's a new voice. Who's that? What the fuck is going on? Better for you to stay up here just in case there is someone who has come to the door. No point in them knowing that someone from That Place is in the house. That'll just be asking for trouble. What if it's a raid, though? Shit. What if the fighters have already found out that someone from That Place is in the house and it's—Don't spiral. It's not been that long since the declaration. If the fighters are going to come for you, it's going to take them a little more time. Fuck. That's not helping.

She takes one of his cigarettes from the pack that he's left lying by the cushions. She indulges this habit once in a while. Okay, fine. More than once in a while. She is stuck in a curfew, okay?

Maybe she needed to use The Glow.

She pulls the cigarette out of the pack.

She looks at it and thinks about quitting the habit.

She decides that today is not the day that she is going to quit the habit.

She lights the cigarette.

She takes a drag.

She focuses on how she blows the smoke out.

She focuses on the smoke and the patterns that it makes in the air.
She looks at the cigarette and consciously decides to ash it.
She watches the grey dust fall into the receptacle.
She takes the next drag.

- I thought you had quit!

◆ I have. What was it?

- The neighbour's car backfired. His wife's in labour.

◆ Oh, thank God. I mean, not for him. I thought it was—

- No, not a bomb or a protest or anything like that. Just his car.

◆ What's he going to do?

- He just came over to ask if he could use our car. He's working with Dad now to use the landline and call the hospital. No point in him taking our car if they're not even going to let him access the roads. He doesn't have a landline. Anyway it'll—

◆ What if he can't reach the hospital on the landline?

- Then he'll probably just take the chance and drive her there anyway. At least she has a condition that the soldiers will be able to see at the checkpoints. God forbid she had something that they couldn't confirm by just looking at her. They'll probably be fine. Start the movie again, no? And give me the rest of that smoke.

◆ There's not much left.

—breakdown. A fracture from reality in which he is unable to reconcile the myriad ideas that were now occupying his head and his heart: the loss of Doctor, the liaison between Uncle and Wife, the betrayal of Doctor by Uncle, the re-entry of Sweetheart into Son's life, and now, the Doctor's desire for Son to avenge his betrayal by Uncle. A newfound obligation that he knew was going to define the rest of his days. All of this would have been enough to break anyone. But when someone is already carrying the wounds of war—the kinds of wounds that come from simply living in a place like This Place—the confluence of so many instigators can be catastrophic. Some might call it madness. A form of trauma or post-traumatic stress disorder or a psychotic break or extreme anxiety or one of the many other named and unnameable conditions that consume citizens of This Place. It is in such a state of mind that the Son makes it his life's mission to kill Uncle.

HOW IT EVOLVED

Here are the strategies I was telling you about. They were written for a particular kind of imaginary audience—someone like me, living under occupation, who might need some strategies on ways to cope. I don't know how you'll be able to try them out in That Place.

Are you planning to keep yourself under curfew for a day or two? Maybe longer? Even if you do, it can't be called curfew, really, can it? To be able to do that I think you need a government that enforces a stay-at-home order. What is a curfew without threat? Or fear of consequence? Or the impending likelihood of bullets flying through your window? What is a curfew without markers of oppression? We need to come up with another way of naming what you're trying to do. Self-imposed isolation? Durational performance art? Embodied research? Experiential auto-ethnography? Immersive empathy?

Set strict rules for yourself. Tell yourself that you can't leave your house for an entire week (or more) except, perhaps, for one designated outing every other day to replenish supplies (see 'The Gallivant'). Turn off your internet connection. Turn off your cable TV. Turn off the data on your phone. Create the conditions of curfew that you know us to experience here, just without the military occupation.

If you don't give yourself a strict set of rules to follow, and if you don't follow them diligently, the simulation you're trying to create is not going to mean much. It will become just another attempt by someone from That Place to say that they understand what we are going through; I worry about the voyeuristic undertones to this undertaking . . . I wonder if such undertakings always stand the risk of oversimplification. If they always pose the risk of being reductive. Is there any way to ever really understand the experience of an Other? And if authentic empathy is impossible, how can the value of the effort be evaluated?

Don't get me wrong. I trust you. I trust you to approach this experiment (experience? enactment? simulation?) as ethically as possible. You know I've admired the rigor in your work over the last couple of years, and I don't think for a moment that you are being anything but authentic in your desire to understand us better. I'm just asking questions with the hope that they will help push your own thinking forward. I think you know that about me by now.

Maybe you should consider keeping a log of some kind, recording the most significant observation from each day and/or each strategy from the Guide? Maybe an outside-eye person deconstructs your recorded entries, to see how your writing/thought patterns are affected by the experience? Maybe you should have someone there do a pre- and post-interview with you, to get an outside perspective on any changes in your way of being at the end of the simulation? Perhaps these interviews need to gauge your changed responses to the same stimulus, whatever that stimulus might be? Whatever the form, you absolutely should consider how the documentation will work. Even if the ultimate audience of those observations is no one but you.

Let me know if I can help with any of the framing/ evaluation design.

You know how much I love that shit.

A GUIDE TO CURFEW TIMEPASS

THE FRAMEWORK

Always sleep for twelve hours. Sleep is at the heart of the whole plan.

THE GAME

Over the course of a day, I spend about an hour (spread out, of course) playing games on my phone. The snake game is my favourite; so is the one where you try to guess which boxes contain mines over others; so is a game of Scrabble against the computer. These are my three go-to games, and during the most structured of my curfew programs, I spend exactly twenty minutes on each of the three games, because—I hypothesize—each of them challenges different parts of my brain. The snake game is about coordination and prediction; the game about the mines needs some dumb luck; Scrabble pushes me to flex my cerebral muscles and to play with words.

On curfewed days and nights that are harder to schedule as rigorously, because I cannot manage to get my brain to function in a desired way that day, or because something else happens to change how much time I have to undertake each strategy on my list, my choice of game depends entirely on my mood. I have found over time that I tend to play the snake game when I am feeling an overall sense of calm or joy, despite the curfew. Moving the snake through the walls and barriers on the phone, watching it gobble pieces of light, weave, dodge, hit the walls, and explode, all of this imbues me with a sense of delight. I can't explain why. It is a game that I like playing when I am looking forward to something. When I am going to go outside for a bit after the game, or I know I am going to see someone I am fond of, or if I know that the curfew was about to be lifted soon. On a scale of 1–10, 10 being positive and 1 being negative, this is the game that I play when I feel somewhere between 7 and 10.

When I feel between 4 and 7, I play the mine game. In this game, you begin by looking at a board of squares that have nothing on them. The first box you click on could be a mine, or it could be a number. If you click on a mine, the game is over (obviously) and the game needs to restart. If you click on a box that's not a mine, you get a number. A number that tells you how many mines exist in the eight boxes surrounding that number. Once again, you choose which of those eight boxes you might click on (based on the number in the box in the middle). If you guess correctly, you survive, and the game goes on. If not, game over and you need to restart. As a game that needs less coordination than the snake game, and as one that requires more luck, playing this helps me when I feel 'blah.' When I'm not sure how I am feeling, and I need a game that seems to require more luck than strategy.

Scrabble is the game that I go to when I feel between 1 and 4. When I am in a really negative head space, I find that I need the most intellectually challenging of all the games. When my head feels like it will explode from pessimism or negativity, making myself think about words and letters and scores and beating a computer makes me better able to push through the funk. It makes me able to focus on something outside of myself. It makes me competitive against a machine that I know is far more likely to beat me than not. And becoming competitive, somehow, makes me a more positive person. Who knew.

I have developed a short questionnaire for myself, for the days on which I am not sure where I fall on the ten-point mood scale. A questionnaire that allows me to score my answers (a = 3 points, b = 2 points, c = 1 point, and d = 0 points) and thus decide which game I should play at a particular moment in time. Please feel free to adapt this as you see fit.

(1) One day, This Place will be free from occupation by That Place:
    a. Hell yes
    b. Maybe
    c. Maybe not
    d. We're fucked

(2) Today, despite the curfew, there is a lot to be thankful for:
    a. Always: health, family, resources. It could always be so much worse. I have it better than most.
    b. I suppose. There are some wonderful things, but what's the point when you live under occupation?
    c. Not really: most of the good stuff is drowned out by all the rest of this shit. How can anyone focus on anything good when there's so much to deal with?
    d. Life sucks.

(3) I am doing all I can to help This Place:
    a. There is always more to be done. Think deeper. Work harder. Do more. You might be able to find a way to help This Place that no one else has thought of yet.

b. I suppose I could do more. I could think deeper and work harder, but is there really any such thing as a truly original idea?

c. I cannot do more. I'm doing the best I can. I'm doing everything I can and there isn't anything I could do to help This Place, more or less than I'm already doing.

d. I'm done. I'm not even going to try anymore. It's all bullshit anyway. What's the point in even trying.

Add the points:

If your total is between 7 and 10 points, play the snake game

If your total is between 4 and 7 points, play minesweeper

If your total is between 1 and 4 points, play Scrabble

If you're exactly at 4 or 7 points, you get to choose! Are you veering more towards a 3.9 or a 4.1? A 6.9 or 7.1? Then you'll know which game to choose.

THE GAZE

When the cable TV works, I watch the news for half an hour in the morning, and half an hour at night. You need to adapt this based on the TV situation in your curfewed land. Here, those are the only two timeframes during which there is updated news about what is happening in This Place. When the internet is down and when everything—including newspapers—are shut down because of curfew, these two news sources are the only way for people in This Place to get the news about what is happening in our own homeland. The irony of that simple fact never ceases to amaze. Sometimes, someone from That Place calls on the landline to say: "We heard that this really terrible thing happened down the road from you all. Are you okay?" To which we respond: "Really? We didn't know. Thanks for telling us."

One of the things that people without the experience of curfew don't understand, is how easy it is to keep entire nations subjugated when its citizens cannot access information. When people feel cut off from everything that is happening around them, when people feel like they don't know what is happening in their own backyards, they become benign. Controllable. Ineffective. Whether this is some Machiavellian strategy that Places like That one design, or whether these consequences are simply part and parcel of how wars and occupations evolve, it works. Nothing is as effective as keeping people closed off from information.

Sometimes, even the news channels don't work because the authorities want This Place to be completely isolated. And during these times, the landlines are cut off too. And during such curfews, where it is impossible to access the news, the external hard drive becomes my go-to. To gaze, through screens, into other worlds helps me see beyond my own.

Keep different folders with different kinds of videos you can choose from, based on your mood during a given day. Have one folder with films that you watch for their artistic merit and entertainment value. One with videos from another Place, in a language you don't understand—just to focus on something other than language. Keep a folder of underground films that speak about resistance and subversion and themes that would never be allowed by the censor boards to form part of a mainstream movie: you'll need these to keep your hope alive. Keep a folder with movies from/about the enemy; they might reveal aspects of their psychology that could prove useful at some point. And always, keep a folder of family videos; videos from curfews past that you and your family and the occasional friend have recorded in the midst of waiting for the storm to pass. These videos can be a lifeline. When nothing else works, when you can't make calls, can't read books, can't do anything else, watching videos of those you love can save your life. They will remind you that you have been through this before. That you will go through this again. And that, unless you are quite unlucky and are in the wrong place at the wrong time, they will most likely make it through this one too. I keep videos of my parents cooking their favourite dishes with no electricity; of my grandfather telling me stories from his childhood; of my grandmother painting a masterpiece, quietly, in the corner of the house, using natural paints that I never knew how she made; of my brother trying to make some kind of new device that he had decided he would try to make that week; of myself, trying to read a book or do push-ups or one of the other things that have made up my curfewed days and nights.

When it is time to gaze into these different worlds, my room is my refuge. Find yours. I suggest picking a room that is in a secluded corner of your house, one that is away from all the noise that accompanies communal spaces. In my house, all the rooms are communal spaces, so to say that my room is 'my' room is actually inaccurate. It is the room in which I sleep and store my clothes, and the room in which I spend the most amount of time, but it is also the room in which my father irons clothes, and my mother plays cards with my brother, and where my grandparents had liked to take an occasional nap. It's more 'my' room than other rooms in the house, so that's something.

It's an unspoken rule in our home that, during certain hours within curfewed days and nights, the rooms that are more one person's than another's are off-limits for the rest of the family. You might want to consider such a rule as well. In our home, because of this rule, we have an unspoken understanding that each individual needs their time to be quiet. To be alone. That alone time is of absolute essence during a curfew, to allow each individual the space to breathe, regroup, and decide how they are going to spend the next hour. For me, that alone time is when I choose to watch something. To gaze. To look into images and music and stories and escape into another world. Letting someone into that alone time, to watch something with them during curfew, is a huge marker of intimacy. It isn't something I do very often.

In the rare curfew during which The Gaze is a shared event, it usually means that something incredibly special has bonded me to my fellow gazer.

THE GLOW

Over the course of a day, during curfew, I smoke a very specific number of cigarettes. So, given that each cigarette takes about five minutes to smoke, I generally smoke twelve cigarettes over the course of twelve waking hours i.e., one cigarette an hour. This is one of the reasons I can't quit smoking. Doing so would make my entire curfew schedule go off kilter.

During these five-minute breaks, I practice

what I call mindful smoking. I really focus on every part of the ritual:

I pull the cigarette out of the pack.

I look at it and think about quitting the habit.

I continue to look at it and decide that today is not the day that I am going to quit the habit.

I light the cigarette.

I take a drag of the cigarette.

I focus on how I blow the smoke out. Sometimes with my lips pursed upward. Sometimes, straight out. Sometimes through my nose.

I focus on the smoke and the patterns it makes in the air.

When the smoke dissipates into the glitter, I look at the cigarette and consciously decide to ash it.

As I ash it into whatever ashtray is lying closest to me, I watch the grey dust fall into the receptacle.

I watch these particles combine with the pile that was there before this recent addition came into its fray.

Only then do I take the next drag and follow the same protocol.

And finally, when the cigarette has to be put out, I watch my fingers twist and turn the stub as its light finally goes out.

The ritual doesn't end there. I then close the pack of cigarettes. Return it and the lighter to the place I always kept them. Then I close my eyes. Breathe in, breathe out. And tell myself that maybe I won't smoke one during the next hour. That maybe I will go down to eleven cigarettes a day during this period of curfew and slowly, over time, work my way down to one. It hasn't happened yet.

Sometimes, especially when I am in the throes of (re)grouping (see The (Re)Group), I smoke more than one cigarette an hour. The nicotine helps keep my ideas going. I don't know if this is truly the case or if it's one more excuse that I have cooked up to continue my habit, but I need to smoke more while I'm working. What this means, of course, is that I then need to readjust my calculations and recalibrate how many cigarettes I have for the remaining hours of the day. I really try to stick to twelve a day.

I've heard somewhere that each cigarette you smoke takes one minute off your lifetime. I've thought about it a lot, done the math, and decided that I'm fine with losing twelve minutes a day off my projected lifetime, when there's curfew. During non-curfew times, I'm only comfortable shaving five minutes a day off my projected lifetime. Those are the numbers I'm comfortable with. During curfews, twelve feels better than thirteen or fourteen or fifteen; during non-curfews, five feels better than six or seven or eight. Completely random choices when it comes to making the momentous decision about how many minutes I am willing to shave off my projected lifetime by smoking cigarettes, but hey, it works for me. It helps pass the time. It helps calm my nerves. And given that, I am fine with these numbers. After all, the other statistic was more frightening. That people in This Place were 71 percent more likely to die on any given day than their counterparts globally. The internet can tell you strange and glorious things.

So, yes, twelve cigarettes a day during curfew.

Five cigarettes a day during non-curfew.

THE GRAZE

Over the course of a twenty-four-hour period, try to spend two hours (collectively) on different meals: breakfast, midmorning snack, lunch, midafternoon snack, dinner, post-dinner snack. Six meals. Two hours; 120 minutes. The big ones: breakfast, lunch and dinner, should take about twenty minutes each. So that's an hour just for those meals. The snacks would also need to be drawn out for twenty minutes each. During all of the above, practice grazing:

(1) Look at the food on your plate.

(2) Divide the food into twenty sections.

(3) One section can be consumed in one minute. If a particular section takes less than a minute, fill the extra time in that minute by sipping on a liquid that accompanies the meal/snack. Time each bite and the duration between bites.

If other people are around when you are eating the meals or snacks, figure out how to consume the food with this strict adherence to time without coming off like a total jackass. Here are three possible strategies:

(1) Don't care what people think. Keep your watch or phone or timer next to you and time your grazing to ensure that you meet the scheduled time as you have planned.

(2) Use conversation to fill in the extra time. So, if there are people around you and you finish what you have to eat and drink in ten minutes, make sure to spend the next ten minutes in the space where the food is consumed, talking to the people around you.

(3) Take your food to a different space, where you can eat alone and time yourself without being wor-

ried about judgment from people who are around you, watching you.

Now, there might be times during a curfew when you need more than three meals and three snack periods. These might be the curfews during which food functions as consolation, even nostalgia, and in such times, you might cross the two-hour timeframe that has been set aside for food. That said, be aware that there will be other curfews during which it will be quite the opposite. When the food will taste like asphalt. When you won't be able to swallow what is set out before you. When eating another bite of food will make you feel like you might explode. Or throw up. On such days, the two hours that are set aside for food will feel like a lifetime.

Day 1

It's been one day and I'm already so fucking bored. I tried The Game, only to realise that I had gotten used to competing with players online. I tried eating in a more conscientious way, but rather than slowing down while I was eating, I just ate more to fill in the timeframe allowed for Grazing. I ate a fuck-ton. The only thing that did work, was The Gaze. And even that's only thanks to videos that the brother of a friend from This Place has downloaded onto my hard drive. I didn't realise how dependent I am on the internet. I need to get more videos from him the next time I visit.

Those self-indulgent observations aside, what struck me most today was my desire to look out the windows in the house. The strong need to, without having my usual avenues to access the outside world, stand by different windows—at different times—and watch the world go by in the same, but different ways. I don't think I've ever noticed the traffic patterns right outside my walls. I don't think I've ever observed the food-cart vendor who seems to stand on the northeast corner for twelve hours a day. I don't think I've ever really looked at how the light changes its hazy hues over the course of the day. I didn't know windows opened out into so much world. Same same, but different.

Last year, a dear friend took me to an exhibition at a museum in This Place—the only museum I've been to there, in three years of visits. I think the series was called "Windows"? Or maybe it was just an exhibit that featured images of windows, but the title was something else? I can't remember. What I do remember is thinking that the exhibit was nothing more or less than one artist's interpretations of how people look through their windows during times of curfew, in places of war. To me, the windows were . . . well, just holes in the wall, with bars-or-something-like-it over them, which people looked through to engage tacitly with the world outside the borders of their home. I don't think I gave any serious consideration to the act of looking out of windows in places experiencing occupation. Could it be seen as an act of loneliness? An act of resistance? An act of boredom? An act of banality? An act of necessity? An act of curiosity? Engagement? Interest? Desire?

I don't know if I'm being clear. I think I'm saying that, then, I saw the windows as being the point of focus in those photographs. I didn't understand that the actual focus of those exhibited images, their core, so to speak, lay in the gazes of the people who were looking through them.

6:22 PM

◆ What would happen if someone had an incident like that during curfew, like a breakdown or something? Would the soldiers let them through the checkpoints without a curfew pass?

▪ Probably not. Not unless they knew the person having the breakdown and could somehow, I don't know, confirm it. Nah, it wouldn't happen. They would just turn the vehicle around and ask them to go home.

◆ Seriously?

▪ Yeah. I mean, there's a list of That Place–approved psychologists. One of them would need to come to the patient's home, check out what's happening, and then issue a pass saying the person needs medical assistance that cannot be provided within a residential setting.

◆ And these approved people can move around freely during curfew? They're all doctors from This Place?

▪ 'Freely'? What does that word even mean here? The approved doctors are also under lockdown for the first two hours and then, if the curfew hasn't been lifted, they are allowed to move. And no, they're not from This Place. As if they'd ever think of one of us as being secure enough to . . . All the people on the approved list—doctors, psychologists, whatever—they're all from That Place.

- What if something life threatening happens to the patient in those two hours when the approved people are not allowed to move around?

- That'd be some really bad luck.

- Fuck. So, after those two hours . . . how much . . . how long does it take for the psychologist or doctor to come around?

- It depends, no? On how many other calls they receive that day. What kinds of calls they receive like . . . how much time each patient needs. Is it a high-intensity checkpoint situation, or a lower-intensity checkpoint situation? There are too many variables to know for sure. They come when they come.

- That's fucked up . . . So, what do people do? You know, in case of a dire emergency?

- Usually each home has a list of doctors who live in a quarter-mile radius. Just in case. Actually, that's one of the things on the agenda for the meeting tomorrow. Making sure that our neighbourhood lists are up-to-date, that we know where the doctors live, and that we distribute the updated lists to each home. Last time I checked we had a bunch of doctors in this area, but lots of people have moved recently. Since the last election, ironically. They didn't want to live in an area that's so far away from any of the revolutionary bases. We should have updated the list sooner.

\\\\\\\

- I told you this movie would give us a lot to talk about!

♦ Fine. You were right.

▪ I'm sorry. I don't think I heard—

♦ Fuck off.

> Uncle, upon learning of the meeting between Son and Informant, decides to take advantage of Son's newfound instability and tells Son that it was in fact the Informant, the one who had been in the detention centre with his father, who had murdered Doctor (not That Place authorities or Uncle, as Informant had told Son). It was by murdering Doctor, Uncle says, that Informant was able to get early release from prison. A nefarious deal between Informant and That Place officials. Caught between different versions of the story, and not knowing who to believe, Son speaks of his innermost struggles to his Sweetheart and tells this former love that he has decided to acquire a weapon in order to kill Uncle. Unable to contain this information, given that Sweetheart's Father works for Uncle, Sweetheart reveals Son's plans to Sweetheart's Father. The news—

♦ I think Uncle is calling you.

▪ One sec.

YEAH DAD.
SHOULD I COME DOWNSTAIRS?
OKAY.
ARE YOU SURE?
OKAY.
YEAH.
JUST LET ME KNOW IF YOU NEED ME TO
DO ANYTHING.
YEAH, WE'RE JUST WATCHING A MOVIE.
OKAY. ■

◆ Everything ok?

▪ Yeah. He's taken the car.

◆ The neighbour?

▪ Yeah. They managed to call the hospital and they gave him a check-point passcode.

◆ There's a passcode?

▪ Today there is. For emergencies that the soldiers are less likely to take issue with like a woman in labour.

◆ There's so much I don't know.

▪ These rules change all the time. None of us ever really know all of them. That's one way they keep us under their thumb.

—quickly makes its way to Uncle, who is now married to Wife, who then tasks Sweetheart's Father with placing Son in a mental asylum, against his will. Not only does Son escape Sweetheart's Father, but he also kills him—violently, mercilessly—before reestablishing contact with Informant and asking for her help. Of course, all hope of reconciliation with Sweetheart is now gone. Informant tells Son that he needs to craft a new plan. And that in order to defeat Uncle, who is in cahoots with the powers-that-be in That Place, Son would need to get help from powers in the Other Place. They are the only ones who would be willing and able to help Son in his mission of vengeance, Informant tells him.

- Are they ever going to stop adapting Shakespeare? COME ON PEOPLE!

- You JUST agreed that there's much to learn here! Wait and watch. There are some fantastic twists that are about to come up.

\ \ \ \ \ \ \

- I'm surprised the government allowed them to shoot this in This Place.

- The power of connections.

- Was that what it was?

- Of course. What else? If a filmmaker from This Place had tried to make this film . . . forget about it. It's all about the director's connections. Luckily this woman's done a decent job. But there's been so many others who have made the most banal shit, all because they had the connections to get the permits to get the filming done. It's a racket.

Before leaving for the Other Place, though, Son decides to finally share his thoughts with Wife. And finally, Wife reveals to Son that she was the one who had shared the implicating information with Uncle. This revelation confirms, to Wife and

Son, the veracity of the Informant's story. That it was Uncle, all along, who had betrayed Doctor, his own flesh and blood, to the authorities of That Place. Wife, of course, is heartbroken and at complete odds as to what to do with her newfound knowledge that Uncle (her current husband) essentially, killed Doctor (her former husband). In spite of her own confusion, Wife decides to help Son in his quest for vengeance. With this change in circumstances, and with Wife's support, Son decides to change his tactics. He still goes to the Other Place, but instead of asking for their help with weapons to use to kill Uncle, Son asks them (the Other Place officials) if, when he is able to gather the necessary evidence, Son could deliver Uncle to the Other Place for just punishment. Son knows that he cannot trust That Place's authorities—authorities who run everything in This Place and That Place and, clearly, are in cahoots with Uncle. Once the Other Place agrees to Son's proposition, Wife creates and executes an elaborate ploy to elicit a confession from Uncle. She succeeds. Wife then sends the recording to Son, who now returns to This Place with officials from the Other Place, who arrest Uncle and whisk him away to a detention centre in their region.

Flash forward one week: once again, Uncle has managed to use his powerful connections—if you have those kinds of connections in That Place, you sure as hell have them in the Other Place—and escapes to a Country far, far away from This, That, or the Other Place. Word of Uncle's escape reaches Son and Wife. The movie ends with Uncle on a plane, heading to Another Country and with Wife and Son at a crossroads about what they can do next to avenge the loss of Doctor.

▪ That's the perfect setup for a sequel.

◆ Absolutely.

\ \ \ \ \ \ \

▪ What do you think they'll do in the sequel?

◆ I think the Son fellow will make some kind of a deal with a revolutionary in This Place who has connections in the Country where the Uncle has gone to, and then he'll use those connections to go to that Country himself and kill Uncle. And then he'll record it all on a camera so that he can come back and show it to his mom.

▪ I don't know . . . I think Son will come up with an elaborate ploy and go undercover in the organisation Uncle is now using to make money in that Country. Then, slowly, Son will climb up the ladder in that organisation and reveal that Uncle still has not changed his ways . . . maybe he's involved in an embezzlement racket or something? Anyway, he will expose Uncle's behaviour and get him in a lot of trouble with the local authorities. Enough for him to be imprisoned for a lifetime. And, of course, while doing all this, Son will also fall in love along the way . . . maybe with the son of the CEO of the company in which Uncle works, or something like that?

◆ Nah . . . I don't like this option. Not juicy enough.

- How about this . . . Uncle is in this other Country but keeps coming back to This Place to visit. It is his home after all. He needs to come back to visit. And he certainly has enough connections to make that happen. Son and Wife spy on him and figure out how he does this . . . when he comes, for how long, where he stays, all of that. And then, during one of these visits, when the Uncle is back in This Place and is least expecting it to happen, the new Leader of the revolutionary group—the same group whose old Leader the Doctor had helped at the beginning of all of this chaos—helps Son figure out a way to assassinate Uncle. BUT the twist in all of this is that Wife has now changed her mind about enacting vengeance. She wants to be done with the drama and she wants to get away from all of this murder-revenge stuff. So, she goes to the authorities of This Place, who are essentially the authorities of That Place, and tells them about the ploy that the Leader and the Son have come up with to assassinate Uncle. And so, now, the authorities show up at the Leader's location and there's a big shoot-out or something where Uncle and Son are both killed. And then, Wife goes into such a state of shock because she has essentially caused the death of her own son, that she decides to take her own life.

- Damn. That's dark. And super dramatic.

- Right?

- Why do you want her to kill herself in the end though?

- For the drama.

- But symbolically, doesn't it say that the woman has no choice to escape the drama caused by the men in her life, other than to off herself.

- Hmmm . . . What if . . . I don't know . . .

\ \ \ \ \ \ \

* What if it becomes like . . . they both are killed, right, the Son and Uncle. And then the Wife realises that she cannot let these men and their drives for revenge control her life anymore. So, she leaves This Place and creates a new life for herself in Another Country.

▪ Mmmm . . . I don't know . . . I like the part where she decides that the men causing the drama in her life need to stop. But I don't know if I'd want her to leave This Place . . . because then the narrative becomes, you know, if you want to escape the sorrow and the darkness and intensity, you've got to leave This Place . . . and that's a problematic narrative to put forward.

* . . . Hmm . . . What if . . . Let's go back to the basics then. The main premise of this movie, its ending anyway, is that . . . well, regardless of where one is, That Place or the Other Place or This Place, people in power will always get away with what they have done . . . they will always get what they want . . . because they know which strings to pull.

▪ Right.

◆ Is that what you'd want the sequel to continue to focus on? That sort of . . . abuse of power or nepotism or whatever you want to call it? Or, in the sequel, does that shift to . . . I don't know . . . the triumph of good versus evil or, I don't know, something else.

▪ I like where you were going with the idea of Wife realising that she just needed to pull herself out of this mess that the Son and Uncle were creating. I think the sequel should definitely become about her. But I don't think she should leave This Place. Maybe she stays? What does it look like if she stays, with this realisation that she cannot be drawn into these dramatic revenge fantasies of other people? We'd essentially be saying that she's realised, what? She's realised that she, in a way, is like This Place. Pulled apart in the brouhaha between That Place and the Other Place.

◆ You lost me on that last bit.

▪ Yes. Okay. So. The first movie makes the point that you can get out of any shitty situation if you have the connections. But it also makes the point that This Place is sort of stuck, as a pawn of sorts, between That Place and the Other Place, right? Essentially, This Place gets dragged into insanity because of That Place's actions and the Other Place's responses and the Uncle's character is just one example of a man who . . . Well, in his case, who profits from this whole mess of in-betweenness that This Place is stuck in . . . That's still a little unclear but just go with me here . . . So, what if, right . . . what if in the sequel, the Wife is now realising that she has become a micro version of This Place? Where she is mired between the mess of Uncle and Son, just like This Place is mired in the mess between That Place and the Other Place. She realises that her life has become an allegory, in a way, for the story of This Place. She is This Place. *Whoa.* That's fucking cool.

◆ So, the first one is about being stuck in the middle in, like, a macro sense. The sequel would be about being stuck in the middle in the micro, individual sense.

■ Yes, exactly.

◆ So, she realises this and then makes it . . . I don't know, makes it her life's mission to tell others in This Place to make sure they don't get stuck in the middle?

■ Nah, that's too idealistic and too . . . I don't know . . . that could never happen. I mean none of this could ever happen. Well, maybe it could, but wouldn't it be more powerful to end it more realistically like, like, she realises that she embodies the condition of This Place, and realises that each person here is somehow a microcosm of what's happening on a larger scale. And . . . And . . . I don't know. I don't want her to do something big with that realisation. I just want something poignant like . . . like she realises that this is the case, right . . . and then writes beautiful poetry to describe that condition of people in This Place. That's what she does. This epiphany makes her a poet.

◆ A poet.

■ Yeah.

◆ Finding beauty in the reality of how oppressed she is?

■ Finding beauty in the reality that we are all microcosms of the shit that surrounds us.

◆ Huh.

- You hate the idea.

◆ No. Quite the opposite actually. I think the simplicity of that is quite lovely. Certainly not something you'd expect to see in movies of this scale. That's a film that I'd like to see. You're good at this.

- What? Making up possible ways in which movies could create their sequels?

◆ At finding ways in which stories could function as allegories for the experiences of This Place.

- Thanks . . . I think.

◆ It's definitely a compliment. Do you ever write stories?

- Nah, I don't like writing. I find it really boring to write things down. Well, that's not entirely true. I clearly like writing things like the Guide. I like writing things that . . . Texts that seek to codify something. You know? Writing that's more like research.

◆ Really? Not fiction?

- No, not fiction. Not stories.

◆ But you seem so taken with the act of storytelling.

- I love stories. Absolutely. Just not writing them down. In a way . . . I kind of see designing protests as an act of storytelling, right? The whole protest is trying to tell a story. It's trying to tell the story of what's happened here from a moment in the past, until that moment in time during which the protest itself is being held. It's trying to tell many small stories too, of each of the people in that protest—why they care and how they care. How far they are willing to go for the things that they care about. Who they want to tell those stories to. So, they have one audience in the soldiers and the cops or whoever are there directly, right? Then there's the audience of the press that's covering the protest and through them, the larger audiences in the outside world who might be hearing their stories. And then there are the people who need to hear the story for the change to happen, right . . . so the government officials who are sitting in the capital of That Place, far away from here, who are the audience for the story—whether or not they choose to engage with the storytellers in any kind of way . . . How did I get started on all of this? Right, storytelling. I think that's why protest design speaks to me so much. Seeing the whole event as an act of storytelling, which has a range of storytellers and a range of audiences and trying to figure out how to frame all of that with the added layer of unpredictability in the situation, you know? Because the protest ground is not the page. There is no certainty that there is space for another word, let alone another sentence.

◆ This was what you learned in the Protest Psychology thingamajiggy?

▪ Part of it. Yeah. The psychology, if you will, of the event itself. So, thinking about, you know, when we say psychology, we usually think of individuals and their psyches. But what happens when you look at an entire event—like a protest—as having a psychology of its own. An event that has layers of narratives and experiences and texts and subtexts and conscious and subconscious nuances that, if explored, can reveal so much about the people protesting and those they are protesting against . . . It's a beautiful idea, I think. To think of the stories that protests tell through their protestors, through the ideas that these fighters are protesting for or against, and of course, through the responses of the other side to that protest.

◆ That's pretty fucking cool storytelling.

◆ I never even knew that protest design could be a job.

■ I never knew that deprogramming soldiers could be one.

◆ Touché.

■ Changing times call for new kinds of vocations, don't they.

◆ New ways to encounter new conditions . . . and the same old ones. Same same, but different.

■ Same same, but different. I like that.

■ Want one?

◆ Let's share?

He pulls the cigarette out of the pack.

He looks at it and thinks about quitting the habit.

He decides that today is not the day that he is going to quit the habit.

He lights the cigarette.

He takes a drag.

He focuses on how he blows the smoke out.

He focuses on the smoke and the patterns that it makes in the air.

He looks at the cigarette and consciously decides to ash it.

He watches the grey dust fall into the receptacle.

He passes the cigarette to her.

She follows the same steps of the ritual.

Until eventually, they watch the object twist and turn as its light finally goes out.

9:00 PM

° Come on, come on. Help yourselves. °

◊ What did you think of the movie? ◊

♦ It was . . . interesting, Uncle.

▷ Nice way of saying you hated it. ◁

♦ No, no. It isn't bad. We were just talking about how it's a great choice for the event that he's hosting about representations of This Place in That Place's films. It's just . . . there are some parts of the movie that are overly simplistic, and other parts that are so . . . contrived. Like they made the ending the way it is so that they can be just different enough from Hamlet and also have a government-approved message, you know? Like, "Hey, look we're trying to tell you that there are different ways to exact revenge that don't involve violence." Kinda preachy.

▷ But for a movie that was funded by That Place,
it's amazing that they allowed it to conclude with
the Uncle-guy being taken by the Other Place. ◁

Only to show that they are corrupt, right? ▪

▷ Ah yes, I forgot that part. I forgot that he leaves
the Other Place and goes to live somewhere else. ◁

♦ Yeah, we were trying to figure out what the sequel might look like.

▷ No sequel, they arrested the scriptwriter last week,
and the director is facing trial now. No one's going
to want to revisit that film anytime soon. ◁

♦ Really? I didn't know that!

Me either. You sure that's accurate, bro? ∎

▷ Yeah. The scriptwriter is a friend of her family's. They were flipping out when that happened because it meant that everyone else in his
family and friend circle would get investigated.
That's the last thing that anyone wanted to deal
with when we thought we'd have a wedding. ◁

\ \ \ \ \ \ \

♦ I'm so sorry that things are working out this way. It sucks.

▷ It does. ◁

♦ How's she doing?

▷ The same way I am. ◁

\ \ \ \ \ \ \

I'm going to turn it up. ∎

▷ It's the only news chan— ◁

° Sshh. °

◊ Turn it down. They're not saying anything that
we don't already know. ◊

Fucking useless. ▪

He tried to distract himself by thinking about
other things.

He looked at the expression on her face. *No,
none of us are looking at you, sitting at our dinner table,
as a representative of That Place*, he wanted to assure
her. That said, he knew that either his mother, father, or
brother would eventually ask her the dreaded question:
What do you think about your government's decision?
And when that happened, she would have to find a way
to say something about the revocation of the Guarantee
without being too simplistic. He hoped she wouldn't say
something too seemingly simplistic like: *It sucks.* But he
didn't want her to get into nuanced arguments either.
Mom. Dad. Brother. Whoever eventually did the asking,
none of them want to hear nuance right now.

He tried to distract himself by thinking about
other things.

*I should add the ice cream to the grocery list be-
fore I forget. And cleaning supplies. I should write those
down before I forget. Mom will need them tomorrow.*

He tried to distract himself by thinking about
other things.

Maybe it would all change in an instant, he
thought to himself. Just like it had done earlier today.

Just like that, maybe they would announce that something had shifted, and that the curfew had been lifted and that life in This Place had returned to normal. And just like that, maybe they would just resume the wedding celebrations with little to no pause, almost as if all of this talk about delays and cancelations had been nothing but a blip. It could all change in an instant after all, and in the next one, maybe it could go back to being his brother's wedding day.

He tried to distract himself by thinking about other things but eventually, his mind's meanderings brought him back to the one thing he was trying to distract himself from thinking about: his mother, and how she might feel about having someone from That Place at her table. His mother was always sceptical of That Placers. Lord knows, she had reason to be. Hadn't representatives from That Place pillaged her land in every way possible? He needed to distract himself.

He tried to distract himself by thinking about other things.

If form and content need to interact with each other in order for protests to be successful, how do forms change when there's always going to be a military presence that's always situated in the exact same way? How can the protest design of the protestors shift and evolve, when some aspects of that design have no wiggle room? *I should contact that press officer and see if there could ever be a way for protestors and the military to agree to different protest formations. So, there's a group of people who want to protest and there's a group of military personnel who have to control the protest. What might happen if the military personnel knew, beforehand, the shape of the event that the protesters would be undertaking, so that they could design a similarly aesthet—What are you even thinking? That's never going to work. Accept the configuration of the military personnel as a given, and then, work with the creative constraint of the protestors being the only ones whose formations and things can be changed. How they stand. Where they stand. What they carry. What they say. How they say it. You know those fuckers are just going to use any kind of attempt to engage them in protest design as a sign of acquiescence. The problem here is that you're thinking of the protest as a work of art rather than a call to action. Of course, it can be both. But it cannot only be a work of art . . . that is . . . then . . . What the fuck am I even thinking about right now? Man, I'm tired.*

° You should try counting the rice grains. It helps slow down the meals. °

◆ What, Aunty?

Mom's asking you to count the rice grains. As you eat them, you should try to count them. ▪

° The four of us do that sometimes, as a game. °

◆ Counting each grain of rice as you eat it—isn't that in your Curfew Guide? Graze? Or was it part of Glaze?

° I'm sure it's in there. He steals ideas from the rest of and puts it in his 'research' all the time! °

Hey! ∎

° I don't know what my son has put in that Guide,
but in the game version that we play together,
the person who is able to stay most focused on
the counting, wins. °

♦ How do you know who stays more focused?

◊ As soon as you get distracted and stop counting
the rice, you have to raise your hand and that
sign means that you're out of the game. ◊

♦ Okay.

And the person who manages to concentrate on
the rice for the longest, is the winner. ∎

♦ What does the winner win?

° The game. °

▷ Nothing. ◁

◊ Respect. ◊

Time moves faster for them. ∎

♦ Right. Ok. Let's try it. How long do we do it for?

°Till all our hands are up. °

1	33	65
2	34	66
3	35	67
4	36	68
5	37	69
6	38	70
7	39	71
8	40	72
9	41	73
10	42	74
11	43	75
12	44	76
13	45	77
14	46	78
15	47	79
16	48	80
17	49	81
18	50	◊ Dad raises
19	51	his hand. ◊
20	52	82
21	53	83
22	54	84
23	55	85
24	56	86
25	57	87
26	58	88
27	59	89
28	60	90
29	61	91
30	62	92
31	63	93
32	64	94

95	127	159
96	128	160
97	129	161
98	130	▷ Brother raises
99	131	his hand ◁
100	132	162
101	133	163
102	134	164
103	135	165
104	136	166
105	137	167
106	138	168
107	139	169
108	140	170
109	141	171
110	142	172
111	143	173
112	144	174
113	145	175
114	146	176
115	147	177
116	148	178
117	149	179
118	150	180
119	151	181
120	152	182
121	153	183
122	154	184
123	155	185
124	156	186
125	157	187
126	158	188

189
190
191
192
193
194
195
196
197
198
199
200
201
202
203
204
205
206
207
208
209
210
211
212
213

Just end the game.
The ladies are clearly bored.

HOW IT EVOLVED AND DEVELOPED

Since you were gracious enough to share your Guide with me, I wanted to do the same. Here are the beginnings of the Curriculum that I want to implement with That Place soldiers who are stationed over there—I'll send you the different sections as I build them out.

A lot of these ideas draw from archival research: material that I have been studying about cults and deprogramming members. The pedagogy is also based on secondary/tertiary-source knowledge. From movies. From interactions with soldiers over the years. From family members who were in the armed forces. All this to say that I am far from being an expert on military pedagogy, let alone how it might be fucked with.

I know this isn't your area of expertise, but you've lived with soldiers all your life. I know some of your friends have joined the forces. Any ideas you can offer would be greatly appreciated!

Please, please, please feel absolutely free to respond as you see fit. So much of this is going to evolve on the ground, once I actually try these strategies with the soldiers.

THE DEPROGRAMMING CURRICULUM:
ESTABLISHING

THE GOALS

To create a relationship between the facilitator and the soldiers who are going to participate in the course

To foster an environment in which the soldiers engage with the history of armed forces across the world

Are you planning to introduce them to the exceptions? The nation-states that play by different rules and either have no armed forces, or have armed forces that are framed by radically different ideologies?

I think it would be really crucial for these soldiers to consider why some nations have been able to carve out alternative paths for themselves—paths of nonmilitarization; paths of reconciliation; paths of restorative justice—whereas others (like That Place) unquestioningly accept a generic idea of the armed forces being tools of war whose primary function is to wield weapons and decimate perceived enemies.

These soldiers need to see alternatives. They need to learn about different possibilities. There's a serious lack of imagination in what they have been conditioned and trained to perpetuate.

It might fuck with their heads a bit, knowing that the institution they accept as a truth can be reimagined in radical ways with the right visionaries at the helm.

For the first few sessions or exercises of the Establishing section of the Curriculum, a commanding officer should be present *simply as an observer.* This strategy is important so that the soldiers can witness the approval of their higher ups—approval that is essential given the hierarchies that shape the army.

Make sure that you set clear rules for this commanding officer! How much can they interfere in the running of your sessions? Who has final say if a disciplinary issue arises during the session, you or the officer?

These soldiers are conditioned to respond to people in uniform and ranking officers, in particular, over civilians. If you want to have an officer present, make sure it is someone you have a good rapport with, so that you don't spend all your time trying to get the soldiers to listen to you rather than the official. The last thing you want is a turf war.

But, you're right, the presence of that officer might well give some additional legitimacy to your work and let the soldiers know that the Curriculum has institutional support. BUT. And this is a big BUT. Your attempts to create a safe space are going to be viewed with suspicion if there is a ranking officer in the room. However much you insist otherwise, the soldiers are going to see the official as someone who is there to keep an eye on them and to report back on their performance to the battalion chief.

Maybe you could have that officer, or maybe even the battalion chief, introduce you to the group a day before the work begins? That way, the soldiers will know that you have the support of the powers that be, but none of those powers need to be present during the sessions themselves?

EXERCISE 1

The first session, and perhaps the beginning of each session in the Establishing section of the Curriculum, begins with physical exercises: exercises that already form a part of the soldiers' overall training regime. Since the soldiers are already comfortable with the idea of exercising their bodies, this would be a way in which to ease the participants into the content that is to follow. At the end of the exercises, the soldiers should be breaking a sweat, while also revelling in the adrenaline from having worked out their bodies.

While the soldiers are engaging in the abovementioned sequence of exercises, papers and pens are laid across the room. After an appropriate duration of physical exercise, the soldiers are asked to sit in front of a piece of paper and a pen and freewrite—they are invited to write about whatever they want, however they want.

They're going to need a LOT more guidance on this. Free-writing is hard enough for people who have the practice of writing. Here, you're talking about people who haven't been asked to be creative for a long time. They need rules. They thrive on rules. And, at least in the beginning, they're going to need you to guide them on possible ways to write.

Consider giving them a firm time limit. Maybe even some themes to choose from? A few options for how to format their writing? I know that might seem too prescriptive to you, but trust me, they're going to need the guidance at this stage.

So, for example, since the goal of this section of the Curriculum is for you all to get to know each other, maybe you could ask them to choose from themes like home or family or hope or ambition or love? Themes that will force them to share personal sides of themselves.

As for the structures, maybe give them something easy . . . like writing twenty lines where each line has one more word than the one that comes before it?

Like
Like this.
Like this piece
of writing that is
quite crappy and yet, follows
the rules of an arbitrary game.

I'm giving you a lot of comments in this section. You need to tell me if this is too much!

At the end of the freewriting, the soldiers should be asked to put their pens down and to share their texts with each other. There are various ways to share these texts and the facilitator should choose an option that seems to best fit the dynamic of that particular cohort of participants: as an open mic event for the larger group, as an anonymised event where participants read others' texts, as an intimate sharing in two-person pairs, as a text-installation-exhibition, or something entirely different.

Regardless of the strategy that is ultimately used, the participants should be asked to make notes when they listen to/read their peers' texts. What are some resonances that they see between their own lives and those of some of their peers, as expressed in their texts? How have these resonant experiences led to similarities and differences in the individuals' thoughts about their own writing? What are some differences that they see between their own lives and those of some of their peers, as expressed in their texts? How have these differing experiences led to similarities and differences in the individuals' thoughts about the theme that they have chosen to write about?

EXERCISE 2

The participants are asked to interview each other, with the following conditions:

- The goal is for the two people to get to know each other better.
- The interviewer cannot ask questions that elicit a YES or NO response.
- The interviewee should take a few seconds to really think about their answer. There is no rush to answer the question.
- The interviewee should make sure that they understand the questions and all the terms that the interviewer is using. For example, if the interviewer asks the interviewee if they "miss home," the interviewee should ask the interviewer how they are defining the term "miss."

When both members in each pairing have had the opportunity to be interviewed, each participant introduces the person that they interviewed to the rest of the group. For example, if soldier A interviews soldier B, at the end of the interview process, soldier A has to introduce soldier B to the rest of the group.

Again, I think you're expecting too much of them. There are going to be soldiers in there who have never been asked to think for themselves. Soldiers who have never been to a school or educational institution. Soldiers who have never been asked an open-ended question in their lives. It is, after all, an extremely suffocated mind that in turn suffocates others.

Why not start by showing them an example of what such an interview might look like? Maybe you could ask two volunteers from the group to conduct an interview, and have like a stop and start approach . . . Every time a less-than-ideal question is asked or when a responder is being difficult to interview, you stop the process and ask the rest of the group to identify why you stopped the volunteers? That way you'd be modelling a collaborative learning space where everyone is part of the learning process. Where you'd also be showing them what constructive criticism looks like, so that they can learn to dissociate critique from criticism?

I know I might be a broken record here, but I think you also need to give them examples of questions that they can ask each other in the interviews. Do you want them to ask each other about their home lives? Why they joined the armed forces? Their hopes and dreams? Their families? You're going to have to be more specific about what you want them to get to know about each other.

If a caged animal is suddenly allowed to go free, without the right amount of preparation or pre-release training, it is unlikely to survive. Let alone, thrive.

EXERCISE 3

It is likely that the soldiers will not get into too much depth with their counterparts. Or, even if they do so during the interview, that the peer introduction ends up being superficial and insufficient.

However, these introductions are more for the facilitator than for the group. Once the facilitator has a basis for understanding why each soldier joined the army, and what each soldier would be doing if they were not in the army, each individual participant should then be invited to one-on-one conversations with the facilitator to discuss the following:

- What was most interesting to you in what your partner shared?
- What did you share with your partner?
- What did you find most easy/difficult about interviewing someone else?
- What did you find most easy/difficult about being interviewed?
- If you could interview your partner again, what else would you want to ask them?
- If you were to be interviewed again, what else would you want to say?

Nowhere in any part of these introductory sessions should the notion of deprogramming be even remotely referenced or mentioned. Neither should the facilitator mention, or reference, any critiques that they might have about the armed forces. This part of the program is simply to establish a rapport with the soldiers. To get to know them as people. The lives that they had before they joined the army. The circumstances and desires and ambitions and conditions and every other thing that led each of these individuals to join the army. What each of these individuals might be doing with their lives if they were not in the army.

This is where the seeds are planted. The seeds that will hopefully blossom into healthy plantations of doubt. Doubt about the choices that have been made. About the roads that have gone unexplored. About the questions that have never been asked and so never had the chance to be answered.

EXERCISE 4

Based on what the participants told the facilitator in their one-on-one chats (in response to a question about who they would like to work with in a small group activity), and based on what the facilitator has learned from each participant, small groups should be created. Each group should be created in a way that allows for some shared experience to exist among its members, alongside differences in lived experiences. Ascertaining the right combination of the two, well, that's why the Deprogramming Curriculum needs a fucking fantastic facilitator. In these small groups, the participants should be asked to conduct research into the following questions:

GROUP A: What is the origin of the modern army, as we know it, and how did this particular way of structuring the armed forces/the military establishment come to be implemented in That Place?

GROUP B: How do different nation-states articulate the purpose of their armed forces?

GROUP C: What is the size of the armed forces in different nations (in terms of numbers), compared to the numbers of the armed forces in That Place? What are the factors that drive the differences in these numbers? How do different nations recruit individuals into their armed forces, compared to the recruitment strategies that are implemented by That Place?

GROUP D: How do different nations help their soldiers reintegrate back into their families and communities when they leave the armed forces? How are these approaches similar to/different from the strategies used in That Place?

As mentioned earlier, I'd suggest adding a fifth group here. Group E: What are some nations that do NOT have armed forces and what are the reasons why such an approach would/would not work for That Place?

Once their research has been completed, each group should be asked to create the type of resource that can be shared with the other groups.

EXERCISE 5

The final exercise in the Establishing section of the Deprogramming Curriculum is a collective one. In this exercise the entire group of participants should discuss, with the facilitator, what they learned from the Exercises 1–5. Based on what they explored during those exercises, how would they articulate the goal of this program?

You know...

I just realised what's making me really uncomfortable about the kind of feedback that I'm giving you.

A few years ago, I met a That Place soldier at my uncle's house (the uncle who used to be in the armed forces and introduced my mother to a soldier who is inscribed in my DNA. That's a story for another day, though). Anyway, the soldier was off duty and we were shooting the shit, and something about This Place's independence came up. To which the soldier's response was: "Look, I'm actually sympathetic to the cause, but This Place won't survive on its own. It doesn't have the capacity to be its own country. Not yet, anyway."

His response angered me at many levels, but at its core, my frustration had to do with his presumption of our naïveté. Our gullibility. Our ignorance. I took issue with his implication that it would take a long time for us to be able to live our lives as an unoccupied people. As if we are dependent on occupation. I rejected his suggestion that it might take us years, decades, maybe even generations, to understand what freedom means. As if we are nothing but colonized minds. I detested his sense of superiority. His patronising tone. His assumptions. His biases. As if we are less than. As if we are incapable of thinking for ourselves.

I hated it when he did that to me, but as I reread the comments I've written above, I must ask if I am doing the same thing myself.

When I tell you that the soldiers will be incapable of engaging with your sessions without explicit instructions and hand-holding, am I making the same assumptions about them that that soldier was making about us? That they are colonized minds? That they do not have agency? That they do not have the capacity to think for themselves?

Fuck.

Your Curriculum is messing with my head!

\ \ \ \ \ \ \

◆ I don't think I'm doing it right.

Remember what he said.
Find a point.
Look at the point.
Focus on it.
Focus on it.
Focus on it.
Fuck, I need to get the stationery to get—
Glaze.
Glaze.
Glaze.
Glaze.
Glaze.
Glaze.
Glaze.

◆ I don't get it.

■ Just try for a little longer!

> *Find a point.*
> *Look at the point.*
> *Focus on it.*
> *Focus on it.*
> *Focus on it.*
> *Find a point.*
> *Focus*
> *Focus*
> *Huge rolls of paper a—*
> *Glaze.*
> *Glaze.*
> *Glaze.*
> *Glaze.*
> *Glaze.*
> *Glaze.*
> *Glaze.*
> *Glaze.*
> *Glaze.*

◆ It's not working. I don't think I'm doing it right. I'm serious! I swear I'm trying!

■ You remember all the steps that I outlined for you?

◆ Yes.

■ You're focusing on a point.

- Yes.

- You're allowing your gaze to glaze over while looking at that point? So that the point becomes almost indistinguishable from all the glitter around it?

- Yes.

- Great. Then the only step left is to let yourself fall into that glaze.

- That's the part I'm struggling with.

- Can't fall in?

- I don't know what it means to "fall into the glaze." How do you fall into . . . in . . . nothing?

- To "fall into the glaze" means you just—You look at that point of focus so intensely and so constantly that the point itself becomes blurry, and your mind exists in that blurriness. It's sort of this state where . . . where you're not trying to think of anything in particular. But where you're not forcing yourself to not think of something either. You focus on that point so intently that, eventually, the point that you're focusing on will eventually begin to alter somehow. For me, the point always becomes like a swirl of patterns and colours and shapes. Essentially, because of how intensely you're focusing, the glitter interacts with that point in different ways and can make you feel like you're looking into a kaleidoscope of sorts. Does that help?

- I think so . . . What if I end up thinking about something even though I'm not trying to think of anything?

- Then you just go with it. Allow the blur and the gaze and the thoughts to wander and see where they lead you. All the while focusing on that point.

◆ Okay . . . I think I get it.

- So, the kaleidoscope I mentioned, right? It doesn't have to be abstract patterns or colours. It could be a visual image of thoughts and memories interacting with each other at that point of focus and creating this sense of nothingness because of the sheer dynamism of that moment.

◆ So, I just space out. That's what you're telling me to do. Be here but not here.

- Yes! Exactly.

◆ Be here, but not here, at the same time. I do that all the time.

- We all do. Glazing is just the ability to do that—spacing out or whatever you want to call it—for longer periods of time, and to be able to summon that function, that behaviour, on command. You know what I mean? Most of the time, when we do engage in that headspace of being here but not here, it happens by accident. Because we're bored or we lose our train of thought. The glazing thing simply means that you learn to control the blur rather than letting it control you.

◆ Control the blur.

- Yeah.

◆ Dude.

- I know it sounds dubious but trust me, this is an effective way to make time pass more quickly.

- Sitting and staring helps time pass more quickly.

- Only if you fall into the glaze.

- Right. Fall into the glaze.

- Trust me. Give it a real shot and you'll see.

Glaze.
Glaze.
Glaze.
Glaze.
Glaze.
Glaze.
Glaze.
Glaze.
Glaze.
Glaze.
Maybe the stores will be op—
No.
Refocus.
Find the point.
Look at it.
Focus.
Glaze.
Glaze.
Glaze.
Glaze.
Glaze.

Glaze.
Glaze.
Glaze.
Glaze.
Glaze.
Glaze.
Glaze.
I better figure out a way t—
Refocus.
Find the point.
Look at it.
Focus.
Glaze.
Glaze.
Glaze.
Glaze.
Glaze.
Glaze.
Glaze.
Glaze.
Glaze.
Glaze.
Glaze.
Glaze.
Glaze.
He looks proud of me.
Glaze.
Glaze.
Glaze.
Glaze.
Glaze.
Glaze.

- How long do you think that was?

◆ Two minutes.

- Try six!

◆ That's not that —

- It's a great start! If you can make six minutes feel like two, you can make twenty-four minutes feel like eight, and then, an hour will feel like twenty minutes. An hour can feel like TWENTY MINUTES. Imagine that.

◆ Well, that's assuming that the experience of time and the execution of the glazing stays const—

- Let me have this, will you?

◆ Right. Of course. Yes. It's a great strategy.

- It's kept me sane . . .

Glaze.
Glaze.
Glaze.
Glaze.
Glaze.
Glaze.
Glaze.
He's right; this is getting easier.
Glaze.
Glaze.

Glaze.

Glaze.

Glaze.

Glaze.

Glaze.

I wonder how long that's been. Felt like a minute? Who knows what a minute even feels like?

Glaze.

Glaze.

Glaze.

Glaze.

Glaze.

Glaze.

Glaze.

Look at me doing it without any prompting.

- Look at you doing it without any prompting!

◆ Has your time-experience-glazing-rate improved over the years?

- What?

◆ You know . . . as you practice falling into the glaze more often, does more time feel like less? Like can you . . . you know, make six minutes feel like thirty seconds rather than two minutes?

- Yes. Yes, you can.

◆ Seriously?

- Seriously. Those last six minutes? It felt like we had just started when I cut it off.

- Huh. I don't think I've ever thought about time in that way . . . as something you can actively choose to alter your perception and experience of.

- Well, you've never been stuck in a curfew before, have you?

- There was that time last year but that was different. That was less . . . that was different. There was that fucking failure of a simulation too, of course, where The Glaze was one of the only strategies I didn't even attempt.

- I'm assuming The Glorifi—Never mind, I said I wouldn't bring that up. Ever. Unless you did.

- I'm not bringing that up.

- Right. First, that simulation wasn't a failure. It taught you the limitations of a particular approach to empathy—becoming cognizant of new methodologies and their implications are of absolute necessity in moving the world forward. Second, about The Glaze, it's best to try the strategy in times like this. When the shit gets really real.

\ \ \ \ \ \ \

◆ I never asked about its history, did I? Was there a specific year or curfew during which you developed The Glaze?

▪ I think . . . well, it's a work in progress. But, I think I consciously started realising what I was doing wh—

◆ You actually have an answer to that question!

▪ Of course, I do. I think I became conscious about what I was doing when I was a teenager. Maybe on my 110th or 111th curfew. I can't remember exactly. What I do remember is that it was an extended curfew. Multiple consecutive days. I remember feeling like I would lose my mind. I even contemplated suicide at that time . . . But then, suddenly, on one of these interminable days, something felt different. It didn't feel so heavy anymore—the time. It felt like time had moved faster that day. It felt like things had dragged a little less. It felt . . . better somehow. I had to figure out how it felt better. Why it felt better. So, I sort of went back through the day and thought about everything that I had done. And then I realised that there was this chunk of time, a huge chunk of time, that hadn't felt like that long because I was there-but-not-there. I was in that room, living that curfew . . . but at the same time, I was outside my body in some bizarre way. And once I realised that, once I realised the quality that had made that chunk of time feel like less, I knew I had to develop a system to train myself to repeat what had happened. Otherwise, I'd never be able to replicate the strategy again, and then what?

◆ Train yourself?

▪ Yeah, I'd train. I know it might sound ridiculous to you, but I would, you know, set a timer for ten minutes and tell my brain that I had to pretend I was here-but-not-here. And I tried to observe what my brain did in order to make that feeling happen. I kept a journal with me, and when the timer went off, I would write down what my brain had done or seen or thought about during that ten-minute period. Sort of like what you did with your curfew-simulation journal, you know? Just narrower in scope. One particular exercise. I would try to remember how the time had felt. Had the ten minutes felt short? Long? And when it felt short/long, what could I remember my brain as thinking or focusing on? Slowly, I began to see a pattern. I saw that the ten-minute chunks, which felt shorter than the others, involved some mention of focus on a point and the emergence of patterns and falling into that pattern. That's how The Glaze was articulated. As Focus. Gaze. Blur. Focus. Gaze. Blur.

\ \ \ \ \ \ \

▪ You think I'm nuts.

◆ No. I'm impressed.

▪ Impressed?

◆ I don't know if I would have had the wherewithal or the ... the ... I don't know. The creativity to come up with something like that.

▪ People adapt to their circumstances. You never know what you'll figure out now that you're actually stuck in a curfew. You might develop your own strategies.

◆ Maybe I will.

▪ Maybe you will.

\ \ \ \ \ \ \

◆ Have you seriously documented your attempts at glazing over the years? I guess I just assumed that the Guide contained all the material you'd written about it.

▪ Oh no! The Guide was a culmination of years of experimentation, no? For The Glaze specifically, I did document my attempts in great detail for the first two curfews following the discovery of the technique. I can show you those documents at some point.

- I'd love that. I'm seriously impressed.

- Come on, it's just a fancy name put on a not-so-fancy behaviour that so many of us already engage in all the time.

- I know . . . it's not the name or the packaging that I find impressive though. It's the . . . I don't know . . . it's the wherewithal you had when you were so young to actually sit down and think about how to systematise ways in which you were making time pass more quickly. For some reason, I assumed you wrote the Guide around the time that you shared it with me a few years ago. I don't know why I assumed that. I didn't really think much about how long it might have taken you to articulate those strategies, or how you might have test-driven each of them over the years . . . There can't be too many people who do that, who approach curfew in such a technique-based way?

- No . . . but that's not necessarily a comment on a lack of, I don't know, creativity or imagination or anything like that on the part of the others. The experience of time is such a personal thing . . . every person in This Place has had to articulate strategies through which they make time move during these periods of . . . just . . . stagnation. You happen to know mine in more detail, you know? If you talk to anyone in this house, they'll probably have their own story of how they train their minds and their bodies to deal with curfew.

- Yeah . . .

- Ready to try it again?

- Mmmhmm.

10:23 PM

Think of her as your student.
Try to observe her without being creepy about it.
Ok there, I see her lock onto a point.
And there's the focusing.
And there's the blurring of the eyes.
Okay, a twitch. That could mean distraction.
Or maybe it's just a response to a fleeting image in the brain.
Good, there's the clarity again.
Good.
There you go.
That's better than last time, it seems.
Is there a way to stare this long without seeming creepy?
Look away for a bit.
Look back.
Look again.

◆ It's better. I still don't—I'm still thinking about things.

■ What are you thinking about?

◆ Not just one thing, just flitting around. Wondering about everything and nothing at the same time.

■ That's fine. Just because you're glazing, doesn't mean there's nothing happening in your brain. You know? Or that nothing should happen in the brain. This is not . . . I don't know. Is that what meditation is supposed to accomplish? Thinking of nothing? I don't know. Whatever. Point is, you don't need to have nothing in your brain for you to be in a glaze. In fact, having these thoughts and images pop up through the glaze might actually help. You know you're glazing but not obsessing about glazing, which makes the glazing more effective.

- If anyone walked in on this conversation, they would think we are insane.

▪ Maybe they'd be right! You have to be a little insane to find a way to make this work.

◆ Okay, again.

Look.
Focus.
Blur.
Glaze.
Glaze.
Glaze.
Glaze.
Glaze.
Glaze.
Glaze.
I can see you thinking about something. Come on, now. Refocus.
Glaze.
Glaze.
Glaze.
Glaze.
Glaze.
Glaze.
Glaze.
Good.

Refocus.
Glaze.
Glaze.
Glaze.
Glaze.
Glaze.
Glaze.
Glaze.
Glaze.
Glaze.

- Time. Good. How did that feel?

◆ Good, I think. It felt like time passed but I don't know how much time . . .

- See! You're getting better already!

◆ Or I'm indulging you.

- I'll take whatever I can get.

\ \ \ \ \ \ \

- Did you ever have curfews in your town?

◆ No. Not like this.

- But something like this?

◆ There were a couple of times. When I was growing up, when riots would break out in my hometown and they would ask us to stay indoors for a day or two until they were sure things were safe on the street. But even then, it was voluntary curfew in a way. You could choose to go out. They wouldn't arrest you for going out. It was just safer to stay in because there could be mobs around, you know, burning buildings and shit. There was no personal threat.

- You could be in danger if you went out though, right? That's how it is here.

◆ Yes and no. In those riots it was, like, two battling sides, right? Two battling subgroups that clashed over some inane idea. And unless you visibly identified as being part of one of those subgroups when you went outside, you know, with something you said or wore or something like that, you were most likely going to be okay. Physically safe. Even if you got caught in the middle of a mob, unless you were really stupid and said or did something against what the mob was advocating against, you know? Yeah. Unless you did something like that, you were likely to be completely fine. That's different from here, I think. It seems like the risks here are to everyone, all the time. That's not the kind of thing that I have experienced.

- We still find ways to go outside. Remember The Gallivant strategy? I try to run a couple of errands a day during curfew. I don't walk around too obviously of course. I still need to be careful, but there are ways to go outside and get shit done. As long as you know where exactly to look for the, well, whatever you're looking for.

◆ Sure . . . Still . . . the stakes are different than what they are for the riots I've known.

▪ Of course. A riot under occ—these conditions and a riot under freedom are very different things.

◆ That sentence doesn't sound like it should make sense, but it does.

▪ You should come out with me tomorrow. We'll need to get things for dinner. That way you'll get a sense of what it's like.

◆ It would be safe for me to go with you?

▪ As safe as it is for me. You'd be safe from the people who are a threat to me and vice versa. So, together, we'd be a pretty balanced team. Unless we run into a protest and the people who are a threat to you and the people who are a threat to me are all in the same place. In that case, both of us would be screwed.

◆ There's the motivation I needed to go outside.

▪ Well . . . let's see how the day evolves.

\ \ \ \ \ \ \

- Want to glaze for a little longer?

◆ It sounds like you're talking about taking drugs or something.

- Well, it does seek to alter your perception of the world and time so . . .

◆ Fine.

- Let's try it for a little longer this time. Twenty minutes?

◆ Sure.

EXPERIMENT #1

Timer set for ten minutes

Post-experiment notes:

Mind focused on a point beyond the window. Eventually, the glitter seemed to gather around the point and create a wheel of colours around it. Spinning. Falling into the wheel of colours felt easy; like the mind was being entertained without having to do any work at all. I didn't realise the passage of time until the timer went off. Watching the colour wheel worked.

Must consider if the spinning nature of the emergent image was what helped. Was the spinning hypnotic in some way? Or would any movement of light around that point have been as hypnotic? Need to attempt this again, but this time, focusing on an idea or a memory in addition to a point in the glitter. Does the incursion of thought or memory affect the way in which the experience of time is affected?

EXPERIMENT #2

Timer set for ten minutes

Post-experiment notes:

Mind focused on the memory of that chat with Mom, through the point outside the window. This time, the memory appeared like a photograph and the glitter pierced through the photograph. This time, what grabbed focused attention was the way in which glitter entered the photograph: through the spots where the eyes were; also through the mouth. This time, although there was no spinning in the direct way as with the colours, the streams of light through the eyes and mouths seemed to swirl.

Clearly, I have a proclivity for swirly shapes and forms in order to make time pass more quickly. Perhaps that is the natural go-to for my brain? To generate spirals and swirls from any stimulus during the glaze?

More trials would be needed in order to determine the answer to the previous question: on myself, and with other people. I wonder if everyone has the same proclivity for spinning shapes when a glaze-type response is desired.

EXPERIMENT #3

Timer set for twenty minutes

Post-experiment notes:

Longest duration yet. This time also, the period in question seemed to pass rather quickly. I wish there could be a way in which to measure, more accurately, how the time passes versus how the passage of time feels on the body of the person experiencing the same duration. For this round, no prior decisions were made around what kind of stimulus might be used for the thoughts during the point-focus process. I just decided to see what the mind wanted to do.

Clearly, I had primed by brain to think about memories, though. After the colours came and went, once again, there were the pictures of memories that emerged. I wonder, then, if it's possible to use these glazing moments as a way to intentionally think about something specific. Like . . . maybe I want to think about what happened in school the day before and use that memory to start the glaze . . . Or I think about a word or concept . . . like 'Occupation' and see how the point focus alters the way in which the glitter interacts with the term and its associated imagery through the glaze.

• How old were you when you wrote this?

▪ Fourteen, maybe? Fifteen? I can't remember. Clearly it was a time during which we were learning about social science experiments in school. It must have been. Looking at it now though, man, this is such amateur stuff. I can't believe that it's this kind of punk-ass documentation that gave rise to the system of glazing that I've been so proud of all these years. In my head, I had been a lot more systematic and a lot more rigorous in how I had made my observations and recorded my notes.

• You were young!

▪ That's no excuse. Clearly I didn't do any research into frameworks or methodologies to build a theoretical understanding of the glazing.

• Still impressive, I think.

▪ Thanks.

What a fascinating mind. To be able to stand outside the self and to observe the patterns of one's mind at such a young age. I probably wouldn't have been able to do anything like it. I wonder if I could do that even now. Stand outside myself and watch myself watch the glaze.

  No way to know unless you try.
  Okay.

Focus on an image this time.

Glaze.

Glaze.

Glaze.

Glaze.

Glaze.

The edges of that image are starting to blur. Like a Polaroid spinning in space.

Glaze.

Glaze.

Glaze.

Glaze.

Glaze.

The edges . . . those edges are beginning to blur.

Glaze.

Glaze.

Glaze.

Glaze.

The core of the image stays the same, but the edges get further and further away from reality.

It's like the image is be—

▪ You're doing it without my prompting, aren't you?

◆ No comment. I was actually trying to think about what I was doing when I was fourteen or fifteen. Definitely not trying to catalogue my thoughts and behaviours in this way.

▪ Ha. What were you into when you were fifteen years old?

◆ Like an activity or an interest or something?

▪ What was most important to you at that age?

,♦ Well, interestingly, that was the year in which I participated in the army simulation.

▪ The army simulation?

♦ You know, when they come to high schools and create these, like, simulated environments in which you get to pretend that you are a soldier in the army and you get to serve your country and all that jazz?

▪ They don't do that here.

♦ They don't?

▪ Here, it's far more transactional. They come to the high schools, but they focus on the economic and educational incentives you know? They tell us how much we'll earn if we join That Place's armed forces etc., etc. I don't think they ever mention the whole "be loyal to your nation" thing. That would be more likely to alienate the kids. Especially kids at that age, I think. Anyway . . . the simulated environment sounds a lot cooler than that. How is it executed?

♦ Well, you get to go to a place that's designed to look like the training academy, and they have, like, officers in the army play the role of teachers. Or they're actors, maybe? I don't know. There are people playing the roles of the teachers in the academy. And each prospective student, there were maybe twenty-five of us in total in the simulation that day, each student is given their individualised schedule to follow for the simulation. And it lasted for . . . I think it was two days. And, like, you're given a quick and dirty introduction to what the food is like and what the timings are like and what you'll learn in all the classes.

- It sounds cool. Is that where your interest in simulations began?

◆ I think so. Of course, I didn't know at the time that I would think about simulations for decades. At the time, it was simply about participating in the simulation to see if I wanted to attend the training academy after school and join the military.

- You didn't like it?

◆ No, I did! I actually thought it was a lot of fun. The whole "serve your country" thing was also super interesting. I really thought I wanted to join the army after I left that simulation.

- What happened?

◆ My dad. He refused to let me do it. Kept saying that I was too young to know if I really wanted to make that kind of commitment, and that if I took their money and joined the academy, I would have no choice but to continue working with them for a few years, even if I decided later on that it was not the right thing for me.

- Wise man, your father.

◆ Yes, absolutely. I mean I didn't think so then, of course. I was sure that I wanted to join the army and it was a free education. I couldn't understand what my father's problem was . . .

- I know it's not that he's not nationalistic! I still remember your documentation of his response.

◆ Oh god, no. He's nationalistic all right. He just didn't think I'd make enough money by joining the army. His dream for me always was, I don't know, something higher powered. Financially . . .

- It's so tough for me to imagine you, the you that I see and know today, as someone who even considered joining the armed forces. Man. That thought is fucking with my head!

◆ It was a lifetime ago.

- Can you imagine if you had gone through with all of that and had been stationed in This Place? If that was the way you got to know us, rather than how you've come to know us now?

◆ I don't think I would have gotten to know you at all if I had come here as part of the army. You know that.

- Maybe you would have been that different kind of soldier you are trying to give rise to now.

◆ Maybe. Or maybe I would have just become brainwashed into the cult and not had a mind of my own when it came to following orders. Or maybe, I would have become that wolf-in-sheep's-clothing soldier that you used to write to me about. Power does strange things to people. I've heard it can literally physically alter the way our brains are wired.

- The army as a cult . . . I'd never thought about them that way until you shared the Curriculum with me.

◆ It is though, isn't it? If we define a cult as a group of individuals who follow a particular leader to the point where they cut themselves off from anyone and anything that does not agree with that worldview—this sort of blind faith in something. In that sense, the military is absolutely a cult, no?

- Of course. Until I read your Curriculum though, I just always thought about cults in a more . . . civilian way I suppose. Particularly in terms of religion; religious cults that have these masters that people look up to and follow. I'd never placed the military in that particular framework. It makes perfect sense to me, of course. This is where your study of postmodern religiosity came in, no? In helping you think through the way in which aspects of religious cults might apply to our understanding of the military?

- Totally. I mean, initially, my interest was more in the religiosity component, but over time, it was the fragmented application of the pitfalls of religion that really spoke to me, you know?

- "Fragmented application of the pitfalls of religion."

- Right. I know it sounds pretentious. I just mean. If cults and cult-like behaviour might be considered a pitfall of religion, how might that understanding apply to a field that seems totally disconnected, right? Like the military, that's the 'fragmented application' part. Where an idea from one realm is broken apart and applied in varying ways to a different space.

\ \ \ \ \ \ \

- What kind of cult would you start if you could start one?

♦ What! No. I would never start a cult. Certainly not after all the shit I've read about them and how they decimate the spirit of an individual only to heighten the powermongering of another. Hell no.

- Really? You won't even try it as an exercise? What about, I don't know, a good cult. What kind of good cult would you start?

♦ That's the thing though. The issue is not a 'good' or 'bad' cult. It's that the very nature of a cult is the giving up of one's individual powers of reasoning and critical thinking and sort of, you know, handing over one's power to the leaders. That's the part that makes cults so dangerous, I think. So even if, I don't know, the cult was all about hugging people and there was no, you know, use of violence or anything like that, the obvious negativities that we associate with cults, even in a cult that's all about gentleness, if there is a leader who is followed unquestioningly, in whatever sense, that's the problem. No one can be followed or . . . or believed in without question. That's sort of the cult mentality I think, that is incredibly dangerous.

- I'd start one.

♦ Seriously? You'd start a cult?

- Totally. We're all so fractured by different ideas and different ideologies and different practices and there's so much infighting. We're never going to beat the occu—That Place when we're so busy fighting amongst ourselves. But maybe if there was one leader here, who could sort of amass this following, you know? Someone who could get all of This Place behind one agenda, one ideology . . . Clearly that's never going to happen. But man, that kind of cohesion would make things a lot easier.

- So, you'd be a cult leader who brought all of This Place together under one ideology?

- I mean, that's the dream, right?

- What's the ideology?

- That's easy. That at this stage, we get behind one thing: ending That Place's reign here. Then we can figure out the rest of it. Instead of diluting our resources by fighting over what will happen after That Place leaves This Place, first, let us come together around getting That Place out of here you know?

- Is that a cult, though? Or a following that believes in a particular objective?

- Is there a difference?

- I don't know.

HOW IT EVOLVED, AND
DEVELOPED, AND GREW

A GUIDE TO CURFEW TIMEPASS

THE GLAZE

This is the best of all the strategies that I have come up with to make time pass more quickly during curfew. A strategy that can be used when some of the other strategies do not last for as much time. This is a strategy that I started developing sometime during my first hundred curfews. A strategy that involves intensely focusing on nothing. Staring at a point, with one's eyes open or closed, and focusing on the point. Watching that point as the glitter that composes it shape-shifts around it and takes on new patterns and behaviours.

Glazing is an active process of disconnecting from the reality of curfew, or any reality. Of suspending thought by actively disengaging from whatever might be happening (or not) in the world around the glazed individual.

To glaze doesn't mean to avoid thought altogether. It simply means purposeless focus. Where emerging thoughts ebb and flow and appear and disappear. As do the patterns of light behind open or closed lids. When successfully executed, glazing could make an hour seem like minutes. A useful skill to hone during a curfew.

Over the years, for when just sitting and staring

didn't work, I have also designed a few different strategies to help foster the glaze. Counting grains of rice, for example, or folding and refolding clothes. Doing a task over and over again created a repetitive motion that did not require too extensive an intellectual engagement. That's the trick with glazing, you see. It cannot be achieved through an activity that demands too much of the body or the brain or the emotions. The state of glaze can only be achieved when the activity is banal enough to not warrant extensive brainwork but stimulating enough to keep the glazer from falling asleep. Though falling asleep, as mentioned earlier, can also be an incredibly useful strategy during curfew.

In addition to counting rice and folding and refolding clothes, here are some activities that I have found to be particularly helpful to undertake while attempting to glaze: tweezing the hairs from the underside of my chin, sweeping, washing dishes, mopping, removing cobwebs, stretching, sitting still with one's eyes closed, doing physical exercise of some kind, finding the sweet spot between something that is too easy and something that's too difficult, staring out the window. This is a list that I am continuing to build, while taking care to ensure that I do not overlap glazing attempts with any of the other strategies that I have put in place to pass specific hours of curfew. If the glazing activities overlap with other activities, the whole hour-by-hour system I have carefully crafted could fall apart.

The trick to successful glazing—to successful timepass during curfew—ultimately, is discipline. Create a system. Maintain the system. And don't break the rules of the system that you have created for yourself.

Could this disciplined, self-created, and self-imposed rule following be interpreted as a problematic recreation of the larger scale versions of discipline and surveillance and punishment and control that compose places with curfews? Could my attempts to so closely regulate every sleeping and waking moment of curfew function as just one more example of how the occupation has subjugated the very minds and bodies of the people in this land? Of course, it could. But, for me, this type of intense control over my temporal engagement with curfew has become the only way to maintain a grip. On myself. On reality. On hope. On imagination. On life.

In times like these, in places like This, that grip—it's everything. Which is why I offer these ideas to you.

Ok. I'm really conscious that the next strategy might make you really uncomfortable and I debated if I should include it or not, but in the spirit of honesty ... I think we can be honest with each other, no? Even about subjects that might be ... risqué?

I'm really sorry if it offends you in any way. I won't ever bring it up again if you don't.

THE GLORIFICATION

Over the course of twenty-four hours, spend one hour (nonconsecutively) masturbating. Buy an external hard drive and create a hidden folder that contains porn. During times of the day when you need to indulge in glorification, go to an attic or basement or some-place-where-no-one-else-goes. Lock the door and take care of business.

Curate a few different kinds of videos in your hard drive's hidden folder and make sure that each video is about fifteen minutes in length. That way, you only have to find four chunks of fifteen minutes over the course of twenty-four hours in order to meet The Glorification quota.

I'm going to need some heavy-duty practice to attain this level of—I can't think of another word — 'control.'

THE GAUGE

Every day, for one hour over the course of the day, try to find a way to understand what is happening outside the four walls of your home. If the internet and phone lines are disabled, and if the television is also on the fritz, you have to come up with a phone tree to gauge what is happening. Since landlines tend to work even when nothing else does, the phone tree might function as follows (not necessarily in the order described below).

Call 1 might be to a friend who is well-connected in the protest circles. This person might be able to give you a count on the number of protests that have occurred since the declaration of curfew, the number of people who have participated, where the protests have occurred, the kind of response the protests have faced, the number of people who have been killed, disappeared, or arrested.

Call 2 might be to someone in your family who lives elsewhere in your land. Someone who was/is connected with the authorities and could find out if anything untoward has happened to anyone in your family or close circle of friends.

Call 3 might be to a local acquaintance who has connections with the enemy. During curfews, call such an acquaintance because they might reveal—intentionally or in naïveté—what they have been hearing from their sources. This could be really benign information surrounding something like how long the checkpoints might be in place. At other times, maybe this acquaintance could reveal precious nuggets of information. About search operations that are about to be launched in your neighbourhood. About particular people that are being looked for.

Call 4 might be to the neighbourhood curfew collective, to ensure that the daily meeting is on track to happen.

Call 5 might be to someone you sort-of-kind-of-know, who is from the enemy's Place. This person might never understand when the two of you became as close as this, for them to be receiving calls from you during every curfew, but this is a necessary ploy. Calling a number in the enemy's territory will throw off anyone who might be monitoring phone lines. It will make the surveillance machinery think that you are a person who has positive relationships with people in their Place, and that perception could come in really handy. After all, aren't occupiers less likely to be threatened by those they consider to be collaborators? Allies? Whatever the fuck traitors are called these days.

Call 6, if the other calls didn't go too long, is to call your therapist. Call her every day. She might need to speak to you too. In Places-where-curfews-are-normal, therapists and their clients share a relationship that is intimate and precious and invaluable. It is a relationship that goes beyond the expected therapist-client interactions. It is a relationship that helps both parties keep in touch with realities outside those curfewed nights and days. You are not calling your therapist for help, as it were. You are calling her to say hello. To hear the voice of someone who knows parts of you that you like to keep hidden from most. You are calling your therapist during curfewed days and nights so that you can remember that there is more to you than this.

More to you than ten-point strategies and designs to pass the time.

More to you than a birthplace enslaved by war.

THE GROOM

Every day during curfew, even when there might be a water shortage or electricity shortage, find ways to groom yourself for an hour. This hour of grooming is for you to, literally, feel good about yourself.

Many people let themselves go during curfew. They don't bathe. Don't shave. Don't moisturise. Don't face-mask. Don't tweeze. Don't do all those things that might help them feel aesthetically appealing in an otherwise unappealing and disturbing time. It is understandable why these people might feel this way. Why caring about how one grooms oneself during a curfew really seems to have nothing to do with anything. But I know firsthand that grooming can help. Like calling your therapist, grooming rituals can help you imagine that you can be more. More than this. More than a curfew. Which you know you are. Of course, you are more than all of this. You know that.

If there is a decent water supply that day, bathing is my favourite ritual. I love feeling the drops against my skin. The texture of the towel as I dry myself, which could sometimes feel like a massage of sorts. The application of the moisturiser—sometimes chemical, sometimes a home remedy that my grandmother taught me how to cook up with limited resources (get in touch if you'd like the recipe!)—that I make sure to work into every part of my body. When there is water supply, it also means that I can shave. When I can do what I need to do, to reinvent my face in a way that makes sense to me. Sometimes that means trimming a beard. Sometimes that means cleaning off every strand of hair from my cheeks and chin. Most of the time, I don't know what I am going to do till I am standing in front of the mirror with a razor in my hand.

For the times when the water supply is low, I have developed another strategy to make me feel like I am engaging in a grooming ritual. I go through my closet, pull out all the clothes that I haven't worn in a long time, and as I try on each one of those items and decide whether or not I want to keep it, I relive a memory that I have associated with it. What this also means is that I very rarely give things away. Because even if I never wear a piece of clothing again, even if I never touch them apart from times of curfew, each of them has a memory that helps me pass the time. Each item of clothing in my closet has some form of nostalgia that comes along with it. Sometimes, I don't know if these memories are real or manufactured. Sometimes, I wondered if I just manufacture memories to go with each of the pieces of clothing so that I can pass the time.

I look at the piece of clothing that I wore during the first protest I ever participated in. The one that I wore when my mother told me the thing that would forever alter my perception of myself. Of her. Of This Place. And That one. The one that I wore when I lost my virginity. That one, when I first cheated on an examination. When I first declared my love for another person. When I stood over the dead body of my grandmother. When I dried my father's tears after another fighter fell. When the first eight-year-old was shot down during a protest. When . . . when . . .

Growing up, I was always told that attention to grooming is odd. That, especially during curfew, paying attention to how one looks is ludicrous. Selfish. Useless. And for a while, I listened to them. Listened to them when they told me that I needed to find more acceptable ways of coping. Listened to them until I realised one day that none of this is the norm. Curfew isn't the norm. Occupation isn't the norm. This Place isn't the norm. And if nothing I know is the norm, why give a flying fuck if I coped in ways that others deem less-than-normal?

THE GENIE

Curate a collection of books that is kept set aside to be read during curfews. Books that you've always wanted to read but, for some reason, haven't gotten around to. Choose classics from your Places. And anti-classics too. Books that are seminal to the particularity of where you come from. Books that allow their readers to understand them in relation to themselves, rather than as entities that are to be compared to an Other.

The books that I have on my curfew reading list are carefully curated. They are books that were very specifically chosen to battle what curfews here suggest: That people of This Place have no choice but to succumb to the rules that are foisted on us by the occupying forces. That's why the books I have are mostly from the past— works that were written during a time before That Place took over This one—texts that were crafted about a time in This Place's history during which there was value in knowledge for knowledge's sake, rather than knowledge being something that was purely necessary in crafting a suitable response to That Place's aggressions. One of the books on my curfew reading list is a book of poems written by the first female mystic known in any part of the region: in This Place, That Place, or the Other Place. One of them is a journal written by the last king of independent This Place, documenting the ruler's innermost thoughts until the day that he went to That Place, requesting support for his kingdom. Another one is an anthology that includes essays about the different ages to This Place's evolution; an alternative history, if you will. One is a play that lays out, in dramatic form, the various scriptures that shape the religious fabric of This Place. I also have, on my curfew reading list, a book that my great-grandfather wrote documenting the last few years of his life, preceding the takeover of This Place by That one.

The books that are on my curfew reading list are the heavy hitters. The books that I've always wanted to read but have been too scared to begin. Scared, because I am afraid they might be written in a form that will be inaccessible to me. Scared, because I am afraid that reading about what This Place was like, before it became defined by That Place, will break me in ways that I cannot begin to anticipate. Scared, because it is sometimes easier to think that this is always how things have been in This Place. That things are how they are because they have never been different. What good would it do anyone to know that things have not always been like this? What good would it do me to know that This Place could have been a different world? A world that now, I can never even begin to imagine? What is the point of reading texts that might open the door to a past that might break me? What is the point?

I have to force myself to read these books. And the only way I can think of to do that, the only time during which I know I am most likely to even try to read these books, is during curfew. When I cannot distract myself on the internet by pretending to search for terms that I don't understand, to only then go down rabbit holes of investigation. When I cannot procrastinate with other things that seem more important and urgent than reading books about the past. I know that I am most likely to read these books during a time of curfew, when I have no choice but to swim in their depths. It is still an arduous task. Focusing, when the mind wants to do anything but focus, is a near-impossible task.

Sometimes, I have to force himself to read by making myself write out the sentences, verbatim, after reading them. I study the lines over and over, and if I get even one word wrong in my rewrite of the text, I punish myself with thirty push-ups. That's brutal. Wanting to avoid the push-ups makes me force myself to read. Fucking up on the reading because of my inability to

focus makes me get a minuscule workout with the repeated push-ups. Either way, it becomes a win-win situation—if one were to define 'win' really, really loosely.
Another way I force myself to read is to tell my father
that I will explain the premise of a chapter to him after
reading it and if I don't do so, my father gets to ask me
to take on a chore that he knows I hate. Like cleaning
the toilets.

Of course, the punishment-based approaches
are not always successful. In fact, they are rarely successful. If I don't feel like doing the push-ups, I don't do
them. And my father has never been the kind of person
to force me to do anything, let alone clean toilets. So,
sure, these are mechanisms that I have come up with
to hold myself accountable. To force myself to read and
engage with ideas that terrify me for reasons that are
justifiable and unjustifiable at the same time. But these
punishment-based strategies are also mechanisms that
depend, entirely, on the condition of my spirit at a particular moment, during a particular curfew. I haven't
been able to figure out a way around the unpredictability of my own psychology. There are some things that
even the most well-planned and executed design structures cannot plan for.

The final strategy that I use to get myself to
read is a recording that my grandfather made on one
of the many curfews that we spent together before his
death. In this recording, I asked him to speak about the
books and ideas and words and images that, to him, had
shaped his identity as a citizen of This Place. Who were
the thinkers who had allowed him to better understand
and connect with his homeland? What were the texts

and voices and narratives that had allowed him to be able to dig through all the muck of occupation and find a centring that spoke to who he truly was? It is no coincidence that every book he mentions on this recording is on my curfew reading list. When nothing else works, listening to my grandfather's voice is often just the inspiration I need to support me through one more curfewed night.

There are always those curfews during which even grandfathered voices don't work. When nothing can get me to read words that I yearn for. And fear.

There are always the curfews that remain impenetrable. Interminable. Shattering.

And during those curfews, well, nothing works.

Day 5

I almost decided to end the experiment today. I don't know what the point is. What am I trying to understand? I keep hearing my friend's warning. That, if not approached ethically and carefully, this will just become a voyeuristic exercise. Curfew porn. Conflictalism (a version of 'Orientalism'). I started this experience with the blessing of partners whom I trust in This Place; partners who have faith in my ethics, more so than even I do. It feels like I'm acting in a play; a play for an audience of one. Well, two—including you. What will you see at the end of all this, I wonder.

Will this exercise really give me a more nuanced insight into what people in This Place experience? Or will it just create the illusion that I understand something I don't? Or worse yet, will this simulation just amount to nothing? An exercise that comes to naught?

It's hard not to wonder if this current state of existential angst is a consequence of the imposed isolation. Or if it's just an honest self-evaluation of my undertaking. When so much time is spent behind closed doors, alone—whether that aloneness is physical or intellectual or emotional or a combination of all of these states—how does one remain aware of the origin and directionality of their thoughts? How does one know if the thing that is being thought is only being thought because of the isolation? How does one demarcate the line between the integrity of the thought and the contamination that might be caused by the circumstances that give rise to it?

I don't think I'm making sense. And of course, I immediately wonder . . . Am I performing a lack of coherence, a quality that I think must accompany solitude and isolation? Or am I truly this incoherent right now?

Being alone during this experience was supposed to be a stressor that made up for the lack of an external threat. But now, I'm wondering if it's the presence of family, the presence of friends, that makes curfews surviveable. So, by taking this on alone, I've not added a stressor, I've simply eliminated an important element in how people make it through the darkness. Is this why large families continue to live together in This Place? Is this why couples there tend to have multiple children? Did these traditions precede the condition of occupation? Or are they a consequence of it?

Also, I have no fucking clue how to approach The Glaze.

11:53 PM TO 1:00 AM

As she watched him leave the room to go share space with his brother, she almost called him back. She didn't want him to leave. Not for any intention of using the night to further their growing knowledge of each other, but simply because she was afraid to sleep alone. She'd always been afraid to sleep alone, but that fear had gotten worse ever since her first visit to This Place. Even now, as she tried to lay back and relax and close her eyes, she kept jumping at the slightest sound. What was that? Rats scurrying through the ceiling boards? And that? The neighbourhood dogs searching through the trash? And that? And that? And that?

As he left her in the room to go share space with his brother, he almost turned back to make sure that she would be okay on her own. Would she interpret him as having suspicious intentions though? After all, he was questioning his intentions himself. He didn't just want to share the room with her to make sure she'd be ok.

He wanted to share the room with her because he wanted any excuse to be close to her and to see where things could lead, even when he knew that they wouldn't lead anywhere. Which made him want to be near her all the more. "No. Just keep your head down and keep going," he told himself.

What made her the most uncomfortable was the fact that the doors didn't have locks on them. A custom in This Place, where the line between public and private space was hazy and every space was everyone else's. It was a quality to life here that she was still getting used to. She thought she saw the door move a bit. Was it the wind? What if the army came on a patrol in the middle of the night and just barged into her room? They had been known to violate people during their patrols. They had been known to indiscriminately use rape as a way to exert their power. What if they came to the house in the middle of the night and came into her room and attacked her? What the fuck could she do?

And so, he did what he did every curfewed night. He made sure all the windows in the house were securely closed, in case there was a protest in the middle of the night.

That's why they had got the reinforced, bulletproof glass that could, if they so desired, even keep the glitter at bay. The windows' strength meant that breaking them would be difficult even if over-enthusiastic soldiers went at them with their iron rods. After all the windows in the house were checked, it was his job to check the front doors. The metal security door that was outside the heavy wooden door had bars with gaps between them paned with the same glass as the windows. Double security. The wooden door also had two deadbolts on it. None of these security measures would keep them 100 percent safe. Both the army and the revolutionaries had the weapons to take the doors down if the family decided to sign their death sentence by not answering their knocks on the door. But these security measures just helped them feel less anxious. Like they had some control over who could have access to their home.

While the reality was, of course, that they didn't.

No. She wouldn't be able to sleep with the door ajar like this.

So, for the next bit, she spent her time exploring the furniture in the room and trying to see what kind of contraption she might be able to cobble together in order to keep the door closed a little bit longer. No, it wouldn't really keep the door closed for too much longer, but it would be enough to make a loud sound and wake her up and if that happened . . . fuck . . . then what? What difference would it make to have some warning? No. If that happened, and if she heard them coming in, she would jump out the window. She was in a first-floor room, but it wasn't that high up and the ground beneath her would break her fall. And then . . . she would . . . she would . . . okay . . . she needed a plan to be able to sleep.

So, he made sure the doors were relocked and secure, like the windows, before heading to the room that he was going to share with his brother. This had always been their thing. Sharing a room during curfew. Guest or no guest. They told each other that it was because they got to stay up late into the night, sharing stories and talking about things that they had forgotten to tell each other.

But it was also because there was some solidarity in having the other sibling around. So now, if any weapon-wielding type came into their room in the middle of the night, there would be someone who knew what happened in the ultimate moments before their disappearance or arrest or whatever the fuck else happened to people here in the middle of the night.

With her contraption in place, she would hear them entering the room. And when

that happened, she would jump
out the window and then she
would sprint to the nearest public telephone. She remembers
there being one on the street
over from theirs. She would
sprint there, hopefully with
no one seeing her and then she
would call the commanding
officer whose number she had
memorised. And then she would
listen to what the commander
asked her to do . . . Okay. Not a
foolproof plan. It still had a lot
of variables. But she had a good
feeling about it. A good enough
feeling to make her feel like she
had some chance of sleeping
without being in a constantly
heightened sense of aware-
ness.

Tonight was different, though. Tonight, his brother was not in the room. He was sitting on the phone in the living room, coochie-cooing to the woman to whom he was supposed to be married. He couldn't fault him for that, though he knew this would make it tougher for him to fall asleep. He couldn't fall asleep during curfew without someone in the same room with him. Fuck. This was going to change forever once his brother got married. These storytelling curfewed nights were going to happen less and less often now, if ever . . . Fuck. Okay. So maybe it was time for Glorification. Maybe he just needed to get himself off. That always helped him fall asleep.

The half-baked escape plan allowed her to close her eyes. To get under the blankets. And to begin to drift. She was able to relax her shoulders just that little bit. Enough to feel that small action release a muscle in her lower back. Which consequently allowed her jaw to loosen just a tad. Enough for her to do a laying stretch that would pop different areas around her spine—a nightly ritual that helped her sleep better.

She closed her eyes and slowly felt herself drifting. Flitting between various images of the last date that she had been on before boarding the bus to This Place. How would that newfound romantic interest find life in This Place, she wondered. Would she be able to adapt? Would she be able to engage with the people of This Place? Would she someday be in a room like this, with her?

So, he took his computer and hard drive and headed upstairs to the attic. Which is where he always went to take care of his business. And in trying to take care not to wake her, of course he dropped the hard drive right outside her door. "Go back to bed. I just dropped something," he whispered before running upstairs. Just in case she came out of the room and he had to explain where he was going with laptop and hard drive in hand.

"What the fuck was that?" she thought as she heard a muffled thump that seemed to be coming from right outside her door. She ran to the door, "Hello?" Was it Aunty, maybe? Or was it Uncle? Or one of the brothers? She couldn't tell. "Go back to bed. I just dropped something."

Okay. Someone in the house was still awake. And for some bizarre reason, that thought made her feel better. Like, if something were to happen to her now, at least there would be a witness. A completely ludicrous thought, of course. Having a witness would not do anything if the army was to barge in. "Fuck. What if the revolutionaries barged in? What if they had heard that there was someone from That Place in this house? Fuck." She needed something that could be a weapon. Even if it wouldn't do much to slow down anyone who entered her room. She rummaged through the room till she finally found a bottle of perfume hidden in one of the closets. She had no idea whose it was or what it contained, but somehow, holding that bottle in her hand made her feel like maybe there was some way she could slow any intruders. Be it from the army or one of the revolutionary groups.

And as it was on nights like this one, when he knew he couldn't sleep and therefore could sleep even less than he would have had he thought he would be able to sleep, even Glorification was hard.

Pun unintended. He would watch the different go-to videos that he had in the secret folder. Videos that he was bizarrely embarrassed of having as his stimulus even though he knew there was nothing to be embarrassed about. Was it the anarchist in him who found it

She tested the perfume. Yes, it sprayed well. Enough to hinder the eyesight of someone who was trying to attack her.

She kept the perfume bottle at arm's length and kept repeating the steps in her head.

"Hear the noise.

Grab the perfume.

Jump out the window, spraying someone if needed.

Run to the phone.

Call the commander.

Do what she says."

problematic that he was pandering to such commodified modes of sexual engagement? Was it the prude that had always been lurking inside him, despite a family that told him never to inhibit his sexual explorations? Whatever the reason for his discomfort, he felt the need to conduct his glorification in the darkness and the silence of his attic, before feeling a familiar sense of languidness consume his body. Enough to think that sleep might actually be a possibility now.

As he walked back downstairs to the room he shared with his brother, he stopped outside her door for a quick second. Just to make sure that everything was okay. Not that he could have said otherwise through the closed door. His brother was still on the phone when he walked past him and it looked, surprisingly, like he was sleeping on/in/near the phone. He'd never seen him this way.

"Hear the noise.
Grab the perfume.
Jump out the window, spraying someone if needed.
Run to the phone.
Call the commander.
Do what she says."

Finally, he felt like some sleep would come his way. And he lay there, closed his eyes, and hoped for a commodity that was scarce in his world. He slept. He thought he would sleep.

"Hear the noise.
Grab the perfume.
Jump out the window, spraying someone if needed.
Run to the ph—"

He checked his phone. It had been five minutes. He thought it had been at least half an hour. Okay. Sleep wasn't working.

She slept.

Maybe glazing would come back to save the day. After all, if glazing was a way to fool your brain into thinking that time was passing more quickly,

She slept. Deeply. Restoratively. Dreamlessly.

maybe he could invent a way to glaze in which he could convince his brain and body that he was sleeping?

That would need a new name, though. The Glade, maybe? Or The Graph? Or the Glyph? Or the Globe? Glading? Graphing? Glyphing? Globing? Nah . . . he would revisit the names when he was more awake.

4:12 AM TO 5:15 AM

She slept. Dreaming of things and people and events and memories that flitted around in random order. Things and people and events and memories that looked like photographs. Polaroids with blurring edges that seemed to disappear into the nothingness around it while starkly highlighting the image itself. There was an image of the first love who disappeared in the distance—their first date that she-didn't-know-was-a-date in the school audito-

He started trying to invent this strategy. This version would begin with the eyes being closed. Focusing on a point behind closed eyelids. And just falling into that point in a w—He fell asleep before he could go any further with his strategy design.

rium. There was an image of her family. A seemingly idyllic foursome in what would end up being the last family photograph that they would all take together for decades to come.

An image of her grandfather's ashes, washing away down the river. An image of him and their first exploration of This Place together.

The photographs flitted through her dreams with the blurry edges of what she would forever come to consider her glaze strategy. The polaroid images from past and present that documented her journey from who she had been, to who she was becoming.

He woke up again. With a start. Drenched in sweat. As he sometimes did. Maybe it was some kind of hormonal change in his body, which occurred in times of stress. Can stress do that, he wondered? Activate the sweat glands? He needed to look into that. Maybe he could ask a doctor? He looked at the phone. It had been half an hour.

She jumped up with a start. What the fuck was that? What was that sound? Was that the contraption in front of the door? She immediately looked at the thing she had jimmied together. It seemed to be intact. No one had tried to push the door open. She took a breath.

He looked over and saw that his brother had crawled into bed at some point in his brief slumber. He had half a mind to wake his sibling up, to see if he was up for sharing some stories. But he thought he heard the quiet snore that he had come to recognise as his brother having fallen into some kind of slumber. He had had such a rough day. He needed to sleep.

What was that sound? She waited for the sound to happen again. Was that it? Or maybe it was that? Or that? *"Remember the steps. You have a plan. Focus on the steps."*

She tried to close her eyes again and to fall back asleep. But it took a while.

She kept tossing and turning, hearing real and imaginary sounds and starting at each one of them until, eventually, she pulled out her phone and began to play the snake game. Down. Right. Right. Dodge. Left. Up. Up. Clear the Wall. Clear the Wall. Wait. Left. Up. Up. Left. Clear the Wall. Wait. Gobble. Snake grows longer. Wait. Up. Left. Gobble. Snake grows longer. Wait. Gobble. Snake grows longer. Gobble. Snake grows longer. Hits the wall. Snake explodes. Restart game. Right. Right. Gobble. Snake grows longer. Right. Gobble. Snake grows longer. Up. Right. Gobble. Snake grows longer. Dodge. Straight. Gobble. Snake grows longer. Clear the wall. Hit the wall. Snake explodes. Restart game.

He stared at the ceiling for a while. Her room was right above theirs. Was she sleeping well, he wondered. Maybe he would have slept better if they were in the same room. She seemed to have a calming effect on him.

He would miss sharing stories with his brother. On nights like these, they would talk about their visions for This Place. What it could become. How they would be a part of making it something different. How his brother would inspire a new generation of artists and intellectuals by teaching at the University. How he would revolutionise the way in which protests could galvanize the consciousness of nations. He remembers his brother telling him about his desire for a family.

To then have a shit ton of kids who would grow up to become part of This Place's new avatar. His brother always had had very clear goals for himself. Very clear timelines in which things needed to happen in his life. Deciding to get married at this stage in his life was part of that timeline . . . If they had had the chance to talk tonight, he was sure the stories his brother would tell him would be about other curfews that had thwarted his plans. Parties cancelled. Exams missed. And just thinking of/imagining his brother telling him stories, helped him close his eyes. He imagined his brother's voice. And fell back asleep for a little while.

The game tired her eyes out enough for her to, once again, fall back to sleep. That and the beginning rays of sunlight that started to creep in through the windows. Somehow, daylight made the situation feel a little more benign. Made her feel like she was more capable of handling what the day threw her way. Of course, the reality was different. Wars don't become less warlike simply because the sun is out in the sky.

She slept. Deeply. Restoratively. Dreamlessly. Floating
in nothingness till the knock on
her door had her jumping up yet
again.

"Breakfast!"

He slept. Some kind of sleep
in which he couldn't tell whether
or not he was dreaming. A state
between the worlds of sleep and
wakefulness. A state betwee—

"Breakfast!"

7:20 AM

Grooming.

Grooming.

7:30 AM

◊ Sleep okay?◊

♦ Yes.

° Always. °

▷ No. ◁

I guess. ▪

◊ Wow.◊

I thought you were talking to me. ▪

° I thoug— °

▷ I thought— ◁

♦ I thought you were talking to me.

I would have slept well if not for someone talking
on the phone all night. ▪

▷ You were sound asleep when I came into the
room after hanging up the phone! ◁

♦ Did one of you drop something outside my room last night?

▷ No. ◁

° No. °

◊ No. ◊

Yeah, I was checking on the windows and doors
and accidentally dropped my flashlight. ■

◆ I was scared for a second.

Of what? ■

◆ I don't know . . . I thought it was someone, you know, an intruder
or . . . or . . .

▷ Trust me, with all the extra-strength material
we've installed on the windows and doors over
the years, any intrusion would make a helluva
lot of noise. It would sound like something being demolished . . . not like a dropped . . . what
did you drop again? ◁

Flashlight. ■

▷ Right. It would be louder than that. ◁

◆ Good to know.

\ \ \ \ \ \

◆ So, what's the update? Any news on the ceremony?

◊ Everything is the same as it was when we all went to bed last night. So, I don't think there's anything to be done except to wait till there's some kind of official communication from the authorities about how long they anticipate the crackdowns to last. ◊

\ \ \ \ \ \ \

▷ Maybe there's a creative way for us to— ◁

° Don't even start on one of your ideas now, young man! °

▷ I'm just saying. We need to think outside the box, Mom. Maybe there's an alternate route we can take to get to their house? I should call her dads after we finish breakfast and see if they know of any tunnel routes. ◁

° Please don't do that. You're just going to— °

Let him ask, Mom. Just in case there's another option, we should at least consider it. ▪

▷ I'm just asking. That's all. ◁

° You know I hate it when you— °

▷ Mom, it's my wedding. Please. Let's at least try. ◁

\ \ \ \ \ \ \

◊ Has he told you about the tunnels? ◊

◆ No. What tunnels, Uncle?

◊ Ah, they're a fascinating system of underground
tunnels that were built between neighbourhoods during the Golden Age. At that time,
because they were such a new phenomenon, no
one had any clue how these revolutionaries and
fighters were getting between different parts of
the city to stage their actions and their meetings and their protests, when there was such a
heavy military presence on the roads. ◊

They didn't find out about the tunnels till much
later and of course, once— ▪

◊ The authorities found out because they managed to plant an informant amongst the revolutionaries. Those guys were initially very careful
about who they allowed in but gradually, over
the course of those years, they got a little bit
lazy. And that was the end of their secrecy. ◊

Right. And as soon as the authorities found out
about the tunnels, they started looking for
them and making them impenetrable. ▪

◊ But before that, before the revolutionaries knew
that they had found out about the tunnels, That
Place would stage encounters in them. The

revolutionaries didn't know that they knew, and they used the element of surprise to their advantage . . . They killed hundreds of revolutionaries that way till everyone realised That Place knew about the tunnels. ◊

Right. ▪

◊ And once that happened, once everyone knew that they knew about the tunnels, there was no use for them anymore. And a few years later, the authorities started filling them in and making them impassable. ◊

◆ But there are still some that exist?

◊ Right. Ones that they never found. ◊

° I don't believe that. I think they found all of them and the ones that are supposedly still active, as tunnels, are just being used as ploys to trap people who are likely to be dissenters. °

◊ Well, that's what she says. But I think there are still tunnels that are unknown to the authorities and only particular people in particular neighbourhoods know what these routes are and whether or not they are safe to use at a particular time. Sometimes, a checkpoint gets set up right over one of the tunnels and then they cannot be used so easily. Anyway, if we find one— ◊

° Don't do anything rash . . . °

▷ We're just asking at this stage, Mom. ◁

◊ If and only if it seems safe, my love. ◊

° I know. °

◆ If there's a safe possibility, that sounds like a great option . . . if it's safe, Aunty. I'm not trying to encourage anything!

° I know . . . these two always cook up these plans that have me on the edge of my seat. °

▷ It's been a while since the last one though, no? ◁

◊ I can't even remember the last time we got into any shenanigans. ◊

▷ Saved by the phone! That could be them. Let's go, Dad. ◁

HOW IT EVOLVED, AND
DEVELOPED, AND GREW,
AND STRETCHED

THE DEPROGRAMMING CURRICULUM:
REFRAMING

> Rather than commenting on individual exercises, which led me down judgmental roads in the last section, I'm trying to focus my feedback here on more conceptual questions.
>
> Right now, I'm particularly considering how you will maintain the integrity of the program when faced with soldiers whose personalities might negatively impact the Curriculum's objectives and pedagogy.

THE GOALS
- To get the soldiers to redefine what it means to be patriotic
- To transition the soldiers from a blind following of rules and orders to only following orders after engaging with them critically

THE GUIDING QUESTIONS
- How does the army get soldiers to follow their leaders without question?
- What are the mechanisms of punishment that are used to program this behaviour? How do you dissociate punishment from learning?
- What are the mechanisms of positive reinforcement that the military establishment uses in order to make soldiers associ-

ate following orders with reward, and questioning them, in any way, to be weakness rather than strength?

- What are the psychological implications of the training mechanisms, especially the modes of punishment, that are used by the armed forces? How do you retrain the training deprogram the programming, without making the deprogramming a reprogramming?

- What are the consequences for the individual when they lose all semblance of their individuality and reasoning in service of an institution like the military? When the individual has been erased, and moulded into part of a collective/machine/blob/cult-of-some-kind, how is that process reversed? What does it mean to un-erase the ways in which we become programmed to suit the contexts around us?

Consider this soldier.

A soldier who was born into a home with parents who couldn't afford to do much for her. They did as much as they could. Loved her as much as they could. But they could only do so much.

The armed forces, for this soldier, became a way to escape the barely enough. It became a way to afford college. A way to travel. A way to see the country. Maybe even the world.

This soldier doesn't really care about why she is where she is. She doesn't care about what she is fighting for or against. She doesn't care about the means that she has to use to reach her state-mandated ends. All she cares about is that the armed forces have given her a chance to do more, to be more, than barely enough. She doesn't want or need anything more.

Getting this soldier to question the armed forces is not... Well, to her, there's nothing to question, is there? For her, the army is simply a route that she must walk down, so that she can continue to live a more than barely enough life.

This soldier can't be deprogrammed because she has never had to be programmed in the first place.

How do you ensure that this kind of soldier finds an ethical compass through your Curriculum?

EXERCISE 1

The soldiers should be asked to write a short letter to past selves, while they were cadets in training.

- What do they know now, that they wish their cadet-selves had known?
- What was one skill that they had learned as cadets in training that became absolutely essential when they were later deployed in the field?
- What is one skill/idea/concept that they had learned as a cadet that contradicted their encounters in the field?

Soldiers should be asked to write these letters without signing their names. The letters should then be displayed like an exhibition, and the participants should be given the time to walk around and read the letters—taking individual notes about what strikes them in each letter.

No discussion.

EXERCISE 2

The soldiers should be split into two groups. They should be asked to form these groups entirely on their own, with no input from the facilitator. How do they engage with this freedom? How do they harness their liberty to choose who they want to work with? Do they come up with a method collectively? Or is the process anarchic in nature? Whatever the case, the choice is theirs.

Group A should be asked to create a role-play/small performance/script/video/text collage — whichever form that they are comfortable with—that replicates what life was like in their training academy.

Group B should be asked to create a role-play/small performance/script/video/text collage — whichever form that they are comfortable with—of an *ideal* academy.

It is clearly framed from the beginning of the exercise that the groups have to create work that is based on material that is contained in the letters. Their creations, therefore, should not be evidence of personal opinions. They should simply be representations of data that comes from the ideas of the group as a whole.

EXERCISE 3
The two groups' creative responses in the above-mentioned tasks are recorded. Then, each individual soldier should be tasked with looking at both groups' materials on their own and crafting a short response to the two creations. This time the soldiers should be asked to identify themselves in their responses, with the assurance that the names will only be used by the facilitator to form groups for the next step in the process. At no point will the soldiers' identifiable responses be shared with anyone other than the nonmilitary facilitator. Hopefully, by this time in the process, there is enough trust between the facilitator and participants to enable authenticity.

Consider this soldier.
This soldier was born into a home with loving parents. Parents who took care of his every need: physical, emotional, financial. Parents who encouraged him to pursue a path that made sense to him. A path that would enable him to find the meaning that we all crave from our limited time on earth. In a context where so many children are not given that liberty of choosing for themselves, he was. He was given that choice. And he chose to join the army.
This soldier didn't join the army because he needed financial support for school. He didn't join the army be-

cause he believed in his nation. He didn't join the army because it was an intergenerational profession in his family. This soldier joined the army because the institution gives him the license to hurt with impunity. This soldier joined the army because he thinks it gives him the permission to beat, torture, rape—especially rape—even kill, with nothing more than a flimsy investigation that pretends to evaluate the legitimacy of his actions. This soldier is not part of the herd. Well, he is hidden amidst the herd, but he's not a sheep. He's a wolf. A wolf who has chosen to live amongst the sheep because it gives him more opportunities to quench his thirst without being noticed.

The visible wolf—the one who doesn't blend with the sheep—is watched by many. By hunters. By the sheep. Even by other wolves. But the wolf that blends in with the herd... Ah, that wolf can get away with so much more.

There is no deprogramming him.

How do you ensure that this kind of soldier doesn't rot your Curriculum from the inside?

EXERCISE 4

After studying the individual responses of participants to the groups' creative reflections on the real and the ideal, the nonmilitary facilitator should create small groups based on the group dynamic and what might be most helpful at this stage in the process. Each of these small groups is tasked with designing and building a training academy for future soldiers in That Place.

- What does an ideal student look like, for this academy?
- What does an ideal educator look like, for your academy?
- What will be the mission statement of this training academy?
- What kind of soldier is your academy trying to train and create?
- What does the academy look like, architecturally? How does the architecture reflect the pedagogy and mission of the imagined academy?

- What is the daily schedule that is followed in this academy?
- What is the final assessment after which a soldier is deemed ready to graduate from training into the field?
- What, if any, guidance does your academy provide about life after the army?

Once the groups have had the necessary time to prepare their proposals, they should be invited to a pitch competition with the nonmilitary facilitator. In this scenario, the other groups function as the audience, and the nonmilitary facilitator becomes the judge.

The facilitator should score each group's proposal based on the following criteria:

THE DEGREE OF QUESTIONING

How willing is the group to go beyond what they already know, and what they have already experienced, in order to really question some of the assumptions that go into the training of soldiers? The more willing the group is to question everything—from the recruitment to the mission to the architecture to the schedule to the graduation—the higher the score that they will receive on this criterion.

THE DEGREE OF IMAGINATION

How creative does the group get in the ideal academy that they imagine? How willing are the group members to push the boundaries of the real academies that they attended, by imagining something that might be totally unlike anything they've ever known? The more imaginative the group is—in how they design the recruitment to the mission to the architecture to the schedule to the graduation—the higher the score that they will receive on this criterion.

Once all the groups have finished their presentations, the nonmilitary facilitator should give each group an assessment sheet. On that sheet, they should be asked to score each of the groups that presented their pitches, according to the two descriptors and criteria above.

However, the groups should also be invited to add one additional assessment criterion that they get to decide themselves.

Once each group has had the chance to score the others' work, the feedback section of the exercise should begin.

Notice that the nonmilitary facilitator should *not* share their personal judgments and assessments with any of the groups. The whole point of this reframing phase is to get the participants to reconsider ideas that they take for granted. What better way than to place the students in the role of the teacher?

Ultimately, the group that has taken the lead in the number of points—totalled from all the other groups' scoring cards—is the one to win the pitch competition.

As an award, this group gets the opportunity to present their ideal academy to the commanding officer who has approved the execution of the Deprogramming Curriculum.

Would you consider designing a pre-participation assessment of some kind? Don't roll your eyes—assessments and spreadsheets and evaluation mechanisms are of absolute importance!

If you were to design such an assessment you'd be able to get a sense of the soldiers' willingness to learn, and their motivations for being in the armed forces, even before you start the Curriculum. This would help you anticipate hurdles. Adapt exercises differently for different personality types. Who knows, maybe you even have to consider if your work is for every type of soldier, or if there are particular qualities that you're looking for? Like a selection or elimination process...

You mentioned a Commander who is helping you set all of this up. Can she help you filter participants?

I worry that you are making a huge assumption in the Curriculum Design—that all soldiers are made equal. That all of them want to learn. That all of those who show up will participate in ways that are constructive.

- How long was that?

- Thirtyish minutes.

- Cool.

- What did it feel like?

- Not thirty minutes.

- More or less?

- Less. Far less.

- See? I told you.

- Yes, you did.

- Were you thinking about something?

- I tried not to but yes . . . I was.

- Like I said, it's a process. It's fine to think about things while you're in the glaze.

- "In the glaze?"

- In the glaze. Glazing. Glazed out. Falling into the glaze. Whatever you want to call it.

- Love it.

\ \ \ \ \ \ \

- What were you thinking about?

- This guy I used to know.

- Oh yeah?

- My first love.

- You haven't told me that story.

- I haven't, have I?

- No. Curfews are a great time to share stories, you know. You tell me yours and I'll tell you mine?

- Deal.

- Deal.

- I think I need one of those to talk about it.

    She watches him pull a cigarette out of the pack.
    She watches him look at it and think about quitting the habit.
    She watches him decide that today is not the day that he is going to quit the habit.

She watches him light the cigarette.

She watches him take a drag.

She watches him focus on how he blows the smoke out.

She watches him focus on the smoke and the patterns that it makes in the air.

She watches him look at the cigarette and consciously decide to ash it.

She watches him watch the grey dust fall into the receptacle.

She watches him take the next drag.

She watches him follow the same steps of the ritual.

She watches him watch his fingers twist and turn the stub as its light finally goes out.

◆ We were so young . . . that's what I was thinking about, really . . . how innocent we were, you know? So idealistic. Believing that nothing could get in the way of . . . of us. I don't know. It's a beautiful thing, that innocence. I . . . I guess I return to that time often to remind myself of who I was . . . who I've become.

▪ You're not idealistic anymore?

◆ I don't think so. No.

▪ You don't think so? You don't know whether or not you're idealistic?

◆ I don't know. I mean, there's a part of me that's still super idealistic. Otherwise . . . you know . . . I . . . yeah. I wouldn't be here and doing what I do. And be considering y—I'm still idealistic in some ways, I suppose. In that I do believe that wonderful things are possible through love. But what's changed . . . what's evolved is the overdependence on romance as a condition of those wonderful things happening.

▪ Meaning?

◆ Meaning . . . I think I used to consider that-kind-of-love as being the pinnacle, in a way. The summit after traversing a rugged terrain. The peak that you reached only if . . . if on that journey, you eventually found a romantic counterpart who . . . that . . . you know . . . helped you scale the mountain, as it were. I don't know why I'm using so many mountain-climbing metaphors right now. Anyway, I think I used to think that . . . that reaching that summit . . . that partner . . . that all of that was essential for wonderful things to become a reality. That's what's changed the most since my first real heartbreak. I think. The realisation that . . . that there are many different forms of connection that can create the terrains and the summits. And that focusing on a romantic partner as the only way to facilitate that connection is just . . . reductive . . . and untrue.

■ It was a bad break-up, huh?

◆ Ha. Yes, yes it was. They're all bad break-ups aren't they? But yeah, that one was probably the worst. Because of the idealism and the hope that we—that I had placed in that whole situation. Believing that distance wouldn't get in the way and that time wouldn't get in the way and the huge cultural chasms wouldn't get in the way.

■ I want to know what the fuck a cultural chasm is but wait, before that, I know I'm being nit-picky but hey, we have time so I can afford to be nit-picky.

◆ Okay.

■ First "real" heartbreak. That's what you called this. Him. Meaning there were less "real" ones before that?

◆ Maybe *real* is not the right word. I don't know . . . maybe it is. I think I meant, like, with him—my first "love" if you will—when it all ended, I could literally feel my heart break. Like. I could hear it creak and crack and splinter and shatter. You may not belie—

- I believe you.

◆ Right. Of course, you do. That's what I mean by real, I think. At least, that's what I mean by it in this moment. That physical feeling of literally thinking your heart is breaking.

- "Feeling of literally thinking?"

◆ I know, I know. I'm not being particularly articulate right now. I had had fleeting interests before him, you know? People I couldn't stop thinking about. People I had romantic inclinations toward. I remember this one girl I was exchanging letters with before my mom opened one of them. Anyway, point being, none of those previous shenanigans had caused this . . . this physical response. You know?

- Yeah.

\ \ \ \ \ \ \

- What's a cultural chasm?

◆ What?

- You used that term earlier. I can't remember exactly why, but I think to explain why you broke up? Because of some fancy sounding thing called a cultural chasm?

◆ Fuck you! I know it sounds pretentious but, I meant, you know, the differences caused by . . . cultural differences, I guess. These huge gaps in understanding that can be boiled down to culture. Not culture in terms of nationality, that's not what I mean, but culture in terms of something more . . . nebulous. Like, each of us is a culture unto ourselves, right? Each of us carries these different marks on our bodies and our psyches that make us a culture unto ourselves. And when different cultures attempt to coexist in intimate ways . . . when two individual cultures come together to try and form one that is integrated in their pairing . . . those differences, they cause conflicts. It's a clash of cultures. A . . . a . . . gap. A harsh distance that seems impossible to overcome.

- Personal differences, essentially, no?

♦ No, it's more than that. It's different from . . . from, like, it's not just behaviours . . . it's the beliefs that create those behaviours and propagate them and—It's the difference between saying that two people in a relationship are arguing because one person spends more money than the other. That's a behaviour, right? Personal behaviours about how two people approach money. But, when these behaviours are placed within a larger context and we actually take the time to understand the various layers as to why the two people in this entanglement have different approaches to money, that's where the cultural part comes in. So, for example, right, going back to the couple where each person spends money differently. What happens if we really look into how these two individuals' approaches are shaped by their families? How were the families' approaches shaped by the particularities of the place that they live in? How did that place come to have these particular attitudes . . . No, don't laugh! I'm being serious! Look at That Place, right. Now, if I had to generalise, people there tend to place an overzealous emphasis on money. The way I understand it, this obsession with money is closely linked to the country's colonial past. Where, if you had money, you got to rise higher and go further and face less shit. So, money was the way to escape their wrath. And somewhere, somehow, that attitude has stayed even after all these years of colonialism having ended, right? Money is still considered a way to escape less-than-ideal conditions. Money is still considered an important marker of success. Now, within that larger frame of postcolonial dynamics, consider my family, right? People who've always had money and who've always been able to escape the discrimination that others couldn't because they could pay their way out of it. For them, their attitude toward money now, that's a direct resistance to . . . to . . . their privilege right? They want to give it away. They want to get rid of their money. Money is somehow less important because they want to somehow . . . I don't know . . . feel less guilty that they just got to rise when others fell. And that has rubbed off onto me. So, when I have this blasé attitude toward money . . . when I speak about how it doesn't matter . . . it's because of that cultural context. Of growing up in a family that grew up in That Place, with its particular history . . . So, that's what I mean by the personal being cultural—and political too, I suppose—it's, it's not just as simple as "personal" differences. It's recognising that those personal differences stem from really different ways of engaging with the world. From really different cultures that are shaped by a multitude of factors from nationality, to income, to religion, to gender. Anyway, point being, our personal cultures were too different for us to function well in a romantic relationship.

- You and that first-love character.

◆ Yeah.

- That can't have been the main difference between you and him, though, no? You were too young for it to have been money related.

◆ Oh, yeah. No. It wasn't about money with him. That was just an example. With him it was, and I've come to see this over time of course—I could never have articulated it this way even a few years ago. But with him, the cultural difference that was this chasm between us, was our understanding of time.

■ Of time.

◆ Yeah . . . To me a year or two was nothing in the context of a lifetime. A year or two apart, before our planned reunion, was nothing if it meant that the next time would be the time that we got together forever. You know? What's a year or two of distance when you have a lifetime of togetherness to look forward to? That was my approach to time. Time and how it related to the distance that was going to be between us for a while. But to him, I think—and I have to guess because I never got to really talk about this with him—but to him, I think a year or two was too much time to spend apart for the unguaranteed possibility of a lifetime. You know? Why would he undertake the challenge of being apart-and-together for a year or two when, at the end of that period, there was no guarantee that our plans would work out, or that we'd end up in the same place, or even if we did, that our relationship would actually last. So, to him, that year or two that seemed like nothing to me, seemed like too much time without the guarantee of a future. So, ultimately, what it came down to is a totally different understanding of time. How much time is something worth waiting for or working for, when there is no guarantee of how things will ultimately work out after all the waiting and working.

■ Right.

◆ Did that make sense?

■ I'm going to pretend I understood what you said.

◆ No, let me—

▪ I'm just fucking with you. I get it. If there's anything I understand, it is how time is experienced differently. I know This Place experiences time in a way that is nothing like That Place. And even within This Place, there are those for whom time moves faster because they are closer to echelons of power, and those for whom time is interminable because we are prisoners of it in a way that others never will be. Different cultures of time within the same place. No, yeah. I totally understand what you mean.

\ \ \ \ \ \ \

▪ So, you were at a distance and after a while you decided that you couldn't make it work?

◆ Well, he decided.

▪ Right.

◆ But yeah, essentially, that's the gist of it. Time. Distance. Heartbreak. That's the summary, in essence.

▪ Wow.

◆ What?

▪ That's a really boring story.

◆ Hey!

▪ The way you're telling it is boring as fuck, dude! The philosophical details are poetic and everything, but I want details. It's the details that make a story.

◆ Is it though? Isn't the story more . . . ethereal than that?

> She pulls the cigarette out of the pack.
> She lights the cigarette.
> She takes a drag.
> She focuses on how she blows the smoke out.
> She watches the smoke and the patterns that it makes in the air.
> She looks at the cigarette and consciously decides to ash it.
> She watches the grey dust fall into the receptacle.
> She takes the next drag.
> She follows the same steps of the ritual.
> She watches her fingers twist and turn the stub as its light finally goes out.

■ I thought you were going to quit.

◆ I will. Someday. Right now, you were right. The Glow is a useful way to pass the time.

■ Go on, details. Tell me.

◆ What do you want to know?

■ Did you lose your virginity to him?

◆ Oh God no! It was a lot of heavy petting and groping and kissing, very PG-13. No skin on skin contact in any way.

■ Seriously?

- ◆ Absolutely not! I was terrified of even the kind of contact we had. There was no way in hell I would have been ready for anything more. To his credit, he was very patient with all of that. Given that he was more experienced than I was.

- ▪ Do you ever wonder if that added to the fairy-tale quality of it all?

- ◆ The fact that we didn't have sex?

- ▪ Yeah. Bad sex equals relationship magic ending straight away. Without it, you always wonder if it would have been the best sex you ever had.

- ◆ I wouldn't rule out that possibility.

- ▪ So maybe you just need to see him one more time, jump each other's bones, and then realise that the sex is terrible, and it never would have worked.

- ◆ Right.

- ▪ Unless the sex ends up being fantastic.

Fuck. Why did he have to bring sex into it?

Now she didn't know how honest was too honest.

Here was someone that she was attracted to, asking her questions about her sex life, and that attraction influenced how she wanted to answer questions.

What if answering the questions in one way caused a response that she did not want, which would be averted by answering the questions in some other way? But what if he didn't mean the questions in this wa— *Come on, you know he's trying to ferret this information out of you so*

that he has a better understanding of what he might be getting into.
Yeah. There is that possibility.

- Have you stayed in touch?

♦ No. Well, that's not entirely true. We were in touch for a few months
after we broke up. He would call and write to apologize for breaking
my heart. Made all these declarations of wanting to stay in my life
in some way. But after a few months, he met someone else and told
me about her like it was the most uninteresting thing in the world. I
think I heard my heart break again. There was no point in keeping in
touch after that. Not for me, anyway. I think I always held out hope
that we'd . . . that he'd realise the error of his ways. This romantic notion that . . . anyway. That ended when he met someone else and . . .
It makes sense to keep in touch when there is hope, right? For 'more'
that might be possible in the future. More time. More presence.
More something. But once there's no hope for the 'more' . . .

\ \ \ \ \ \ \

- Do you know where he is now? And what he's doing?

♦ No idea. I heard a rumour that he's become some kind of warrior.

- A warrior.

♦ Yeah.

- Like in the army?

♦ No, no. Like a warrior for a cause. The equivalent of a fighter here, I
suppose. I don't know what cause he's fighting for. But if my sources

are to be believed, he's on the frontlines. Fighting for something that he believes in. Whatever that something is.

- That's why you're obsessed with warriors, huh?

♦ ... I want to say that you're wrong, but ... maybe you're right. Maybe we're always attracted to different versions of the same people. Even then he was a warrior, a fighter, an idealist, and I remember those qualities being the ones that immediately drew me to him.

- That's certainly been my experience too. The different-versions-of-the-same-people thing.

♦ Yeah?

- Yeah. My first—It's tough to talk about any of this without sounding like a complete sap, isn't it?

♦ Yup. It's fine. You can be sappy. I promise to try not to roll my eyes.

- He was ... beautiful. Vital. Passionate about the cause. If anything happened, he would be the first person on the streets. Out there. Fighting. I guess I have a warrior preference too. Fighters are fucking sexy.

♦ Figures. How did you meet?

- At a protest. It was that phase I was in—I think I've told you about that, no? When I believed that participating in protests was what I could do to help the cause? I think it lasted a few months. My absolute belief that stones and weapons and fights could do what discussions and laws and diplomacy couldn't. Sometimes I wish I still had that belief ... Anyway, it was in this phase that I met him.

◆ Love at first sight?

▪ Something like that. Certainly, an immediate attraction. Now that I think about it, I think it was because I saw the kind of fire in him that I wish I had.

◆ Come on now, you have plenty of fire yourself.

▪ No. Yes. I do. But not like that. Not that kind of fire that could burn you with its intensity, you know? Where the gaze, the brilliance of that gaze, it's paralysing in its force. I don't have that.

◆ I disagree. But let's not get stuck on that. He sounds fantastic.

▪ Yeah. He was pretty fucking fantastic.

◆ So, what happened?

▪ What happens to any young person here who has that kind of fire.

◆ Prison?

▪ Death.

◆ Oh.

▪ Yeah.

◆ Shit.

▪ Yeah.

He hadn't thought about that in a while. That death. The starkness of that death. The reality of it. The finality of it.

Death can do that: bring things to a close in a way that another end-to-relationship cannot, when the parties involved in the ending relationship remain living.

In a weird way, this made the story of his first love all the more dramatic. All the more jaw-dropping. He could see that it had some of that effect on her.

He hadn't th—

◆ How long had you been together?

▪ A year or so.

◆ Damn.

▪ Yeah.

◆ Sorry.

▪ Yeah.

◆ He'd be proud of what you're doing now.

▪ I don't know . . .

◆ No?

- It's not the fight really, is it? It's . . . What I do is related to the fight, of course. It's . . . it's the choreography of the fight, if you will. And that's needed. And there's value to that. The choreography is important. But there's still a distance with what I'm doing. A chasm between what me and the folks who are on the streets with their stones and their fire. I think he'd be disappointed that I'm not in that kind of fight. He'd be disappointed that I'm not getting my hands dirty.

- Why are you being so hard on yourself?

- I'm not! It's not a criticism of myself. It's just—That's not the point anyway. I'm just saying that there's a difference between the levels of fight that one is willing to take on in This Place. The fights that happen behind closed doors. The fights that allow you to be a part of them, while keeping yourself apart from their messiness. There are the fights that happen out in the battlefield, in the streets, steps away from the men in uniform. There are the fights that are covered in the blood and the guts and the viscera of the whole fucking thing. Where you cannot be apart from it. Where you're in till, till you're taken out. He believed in that kind of fight. The blood and guts and viscera kind. I don't. I don't want the mess. I don't really believe in the mess. I know that the mess going to happen and that I try to make the mess as clean as it can be. I make the mess less messy. You know? But I'm not *in* the mess.

\ \ \ \ \ \ \

- You want one?

  He pulls the cigarette out of the pack.
  He looks at it and thinks about quitting the habit.
  He decides that today is not the day that he is going to quit the habit.

He lights the cigarette.

He takes a drag.

He focuses on how he blows the smoke out.

He focuses on the smoke and the patterns that it makes in the air.

He looks at the cigarette and consciously decides to ash it.

He watches the grey dust fall into the receptacle.

He takes the next drag.

He follows the same steps of the ritual.

He watches his fingers twist and turn the stub as its light finally goes out.

- So, maybe that was the cultural difference between us. The kind of difference that you were talking about. The personal cultural chasm thing. We were together when he was killed but even if he had . . . you know . . . survived . . . I don't think we would have made it as a couple for much longer. The cracks were beginning to show already.

♦ Because you believed in different kinds of fight?

- Yup. Because we believed in different hows. How the fight should be fought. This singular topic, the approach or . . . the decision or the choice or whatever you want to call it about how one fights in This Place. That singular question has destroyed so many relationships. What kind of fight one believes in. How one decides to engage with the cause of liberating This Place. That one thing defines so much of how lives and relationships evolve in This Place. How you choose to fight, or not fight, impacts who you meet. It impacts who you fall in love with. It impacts whether or not you stay in love. It impacts who you decide to part from and who you decide to keep around. It all comes down to that. What kind of fight do you believe in. How do you fight for This Place.

♦ I wonder what kind of fighter I would have been if I'd grown up here.

■ I think you would have been like him.

◆ Really?

■ I think you'd have wanted to get your hands dirty.

◆ I don't know . . . If you're right, we would have failed as romantic partners.

■ Well, it's a good thing you didn't grow up here then.

> *That was a good line.*
> *Stop smiling.*
> *You look like a fool.*

◆ Did the family meet him?

■ Oh god, no.

◆ Why?

■ They would never have approved.

◆ Because he was a . . . ?

■ A get-your-hands-dirty kind of fighter. They would never have been comfortable with my being with someone who was so in the thick of things. They almost disowned me during that phase, when I was going out into the protests.

◆ But they seem so fine with it now.

- It's taken a long time. And even now, they're fine with it because of the distance, you know? If I had continued on the more violent path—the path that he was on—I think they would have disowned me.

◆ Come on.

- What?

◆ They would never do something like that.

- Of course, they would. Like I said . . . the way people choose to fight has destroyed many a relationship in This Place. And that includes all kinds of relationships, not just romantic ones.

◆ They would have disowned you for—

- Picking up a stone. Picking up a gun. Anything that involved a weapon of any kind.

◆ But what you do now—

- I know. It's still supporting the fight. There's still weapons in the fight. But I'm not the one lifting those weapons. And that's what they choose to focus on. What they choose to focus on is the fact that my orchestration of protests, if I can call it that, helps keep people safer than they would be without my design.

◆ But you're still helping the fight. So, isn't it a distinction without a difference? Like a, I don't know, political leader within a militia organisation? She might never pick up a gun herself, but she knows what her people are doing.

▪ Absolutely. She's complicit too. Of course, she is. As am I. But to the family, there's a huge difference between what I do and what he used to do. Would have done.

◆ Are you . . . oh god, never mind.

▪ No, what?

◆ No, it's stupid. I was going to ask if you're still in touch with him and realised that—

▪ Right.

\ \ \ \ \ \ \

◆ I'm sorry.

▪ Me too.

◆ It's hard enough to have a first love that doesn't work with all the images you have in your head of what, you know, what first loves are supposed to be like. But this . . . this seems far more . . .

▪ Stark.

◆ Yeah.

▪ Yeah.

◆ . . .

Welcome to This Place, right? ▪

◆ Wasn't Aunty a get-your-hands-dirty kind of fighter in her youth?

She's told you about that, huh? ■

◆ Yeah. She mentioned it as an offhand comment, but I remember it because it seemed so . . .

Unlike who she is now? ■

◆ Yeah.

Yeah. ■

◆ Do you think sh—

I don't want to talk about her stuff right now. ■

◆ Okay.

I'm sure it'll come up later and— ■

◆ Don't worry about it. It's absolutely fine. You're not obliged to tell me everything that I ask you about.

Right. It's not personal. ■

◆ I know.

Well, it is personal in that it is personal to Mom, and I don't know if she'd be ok with . . . I don't know. I don't
want to— ■

◆ Hey. Look at me. It's fine. Really. No explanations needed.

\ \ \ \ \ \ \

- Fuck, we have had such different lives.

◆ I know.

- Thank you.

◆ For what?

- For not . . . for not, you know, for being you, I guess. Thank you for being you.

◆ Come on. We're past that, no?

- Yeah. I guess we are.

\ \ \ \ \ \ \

◆ Stop it.

- What?

◆ Stop looking at me like that.

- With gratitude?

◆ You know what I mean.

- I can't help it can I?

◆ You're not trying very hard.

■ That's what you think. It's taking everything for me not to—

◆ Let's not go there. Please.

■ We're going to have to talk about it at some point.

◆ And we will. At some point. Just not now. Just like the story about your mom. It's not the right time just now. I just—I'm scared to have that conversation.

■ Scared?

◆ Not entirely the right word. But you know. Scared. Nervous. Excited.

■ Excited, huh?

◆ Stop it!

■ You're the one who said they were excited!

◆ Well, yes. But, just. Let's table this for now, please?

■ Okay.

◆ Okay.

There was a very particular way in which she blew the cigarette smoke. Lips pursed, the smoke blowing back up into her nose. A double dose that seemed to pepper her nose with little black spots that grew in number every so often. She had no idea that she blew out smoke this way, or that she had a slowly increasing number of black spots on her nose, but he had watched her enough to know these habits and these quirks and these characteristics. He had watched them long enough to know them, be annoyed by them, and still, find them completely endearing.

He would never tell her that he noticed these details, of course. To say so would make the unsaid all the more obvious. Telling her the extent of everything he noticed about her would be tantamount to a confession. A declaration. A love song. And like she had said, it wasn't the right time for that.

There were things he needed to tell her. Things she needed to know about him, about his mother, about their family. Things that could—would, probably—blow up their unarticulated relationship even before it started.

There was a charm to the mystery. To the knowing-but-not-knowing. To the almost-brushing of their hands that they both pretended not to notice. To the gaze that was held for a few seconds longer than it ought to be, creating a visible intimacy—a connection that anyone who was around them could perceive within seconds. A gaze that spoke volumes.

Being stuck in this room together was, in many ways, what both of them wanted. It was a way in which they were forced to sit together, in the same space, without making excuses about the errands they had to run or the other people that they had to meet or the other places that they had to be—all of which were excuses that each of them had used in the past to deflect from the weight of what was unspoken between them. And yet, being stuck in this room was not what either of them wanted. In his Place, and in hers, people did not talk about such things. In This Place and That Place, the precursors to a romantic liaison were not to be spoken about. Not directly. In the Places that the two of them came from, actions mattered more. A graze mattered more than an oral declaration. A held gaze said a lot more than the lengthiest of conversations. So, as much as they loved having all this time together, stuck alone during curfew, each of them was terrified about being alone with the other for an unknown duration, under stressful conditions. There is nothing like a combination of stress and time to force conversations that might be better left in the realm of the unspoken.

Another truth of the matter was that nothing needed to be said. They already knew the important things. They knew that they were two people who were deeply connected to each other. They knew that they were two people who shared the kind of bond that defies logic. And, in their defence, part of their inaction stemmed from a genuine uncertainty about the kind of connection that they shared. Could they assume that their connection was romantic? Sexual? Should they? Or was that a limitation in their worldview? A worldview which held that if two people were attracted to the gender of the person that they shared a deep connection with, that the connection had nowhere to go but to the plane of romance? Couldn't their connection be defined by something other than sex and desire? Couldn't their bond be one that was driven by a cause? By ideals? By the dreams of a better tomorrow for This Place? Maybe they were political-life-partners, or ideological-lovers. Connected. Fused. Through bonds-as-strong-as-romance that also had nothing to do with it.

In the completely uncanny and unspoken call-and-response that had come to define their way of connecting with each other, they looked up at the same time.

Caught each other's eye.

One of those gazes that made her need to pee and made him want to keep gazing some more.

This time, there was no need to look away. They had already begun some kind of conversation. There was no one else around. They could gaze into the other for as long as they wanted to. As long as they needed to. To decipher from irises and pupils and blinks and creases and tears and twinkles, what words might never be able to tell them.

And they did all of that, as they looked into each other.

There were smiles and tears and sighs and blinks and giggles and blushes. Entire conversations took place in that gaze. As they tried to figure out what they wanted from each other. What they needed from each other. What the world needed from them.

They heard the phone ring in the background as their eyes held. They heard raised voices filter in from downstairs. Their gaze still held. They heard something fall and break. They didn't look away. If there was something that they needed to know, someone would knock. Someone would come up. Someone would tell them. And then, when they had absolutely no choice, they would look away from each other.

Until then, though, they had to keep looking. Gazing. Watching. Wondering. They had to do this till both of them came to a realisation of what they wanted from each other. Of what they needed from each other. Without saying a word, hoping against all hope that their nonverbal epiphanies were the same.

Some things, of course, need to be discussed to ensure that they're being understood in the same way. Some things, while beautiful to explore without the pressure for words, need verbal assistance.

They knew that.

They knew that the gazing would have to come to an end at some point. A point at which one of them might have to say what had been gleaned from that gazing.

Unless what the gazing revealed was that nothing needed to be said.

Wouldn't that be something?

◆ I need to pee.

HOW IT EVOLVED, AND DEVELOPED, AND GREW, AND STRETCHED, AND PUSHED

A GUIDE TO CURFEW TIMEPASS

THE (RE)GROUP

This is the time during which I do the homework that is given to me during a planning meeting. I begin by recapping, for myself, the answers that we established to this question: What were the goals of this protest? Then, I get into the design process—one that I have crafted over time to heighten the use of design and aesthetic thinking in the creation of effective protests that were more likely to achieve their goals. Obviously you will have to adapt this (re)group time to fit whatever it is you are working on. I offer my experience here, as a framework.

STEP 1: WITH THE GOALS IN MIND, WHAT IS THE CONTENT?

While all protests might be said to have the same larger goal—ending That Place's occupation of This Place—the specific focus of each protest is always different. Sometimes, the content has to do with the enactment of a specific law or policy. Sometimes, the content has to do with the behaviour of the soldiers. Sometimes, the content seeks to create a connection with civilians in That Place. Sometimes, the content is about the dreams of the youth of This Place. Sometimes, the content is about the lack of access to water in a particular locality. The content always relates to the occupation, but through the guise of a range of subtopics. Do we want content that draws from personal narratives of people in the neighbourhood? Do we want material from research that we have access to, through the local University libraries? Do we want to generate original material that responds to the main topic of the protest through creative expression? How is the content going to be generated?

STEP 2: WITH THE GOALS IN MIND, WHAT IS THE FORM?

Most people think of protests as all being the same. That a protest is a group of people who get together, en masse, screaming and chanting and picketing as a mob. And sure, that is absolutely one form of protest. But my job, as a protest designer, is to give the organisers of the protest—the ones who would actually be rallying the troops and doing the protesting—a range of options surrounding what kind of protest might best fit the content and the goals of the event in question.

Some protests still need a group, en masse, holding signs. Chanting slogans. A crowd of people with no leaders and no followers. An anarchic get-together, of sorts, where certain agreements might be in place: no violence, for instance, or no speech (a silent protest) or a hunger strike or something of the kind. Other protests might need a leader with a large crowd.

Someone who would be the face of the protest. Who would talk or mentor or lead the sloganeering. A leader who would walk at the front of the line. Who would be the first to be arrested? Who would take the fall for all those who functioned as supporters of a particular ideology? Some protests needed a leader with a small crowd. Where, even though there is a leader who functions as the face of the event and leads from front, there is a small group that gathers around this leader. This design is useful when there needs to be more control over messaging and content. When all protestors need to be on the exact same page about what is being said and how it is being said. Small groups, with or without a leader, are also preferable protest forms when the event might incorporate a creative form. Like a flash mob, for example, where dance is used as a means through which to communicate the content of the protest. Or a choir-type protest, where different groups of the protest attenders sing in parts in order to come together in unison. Of course, collective singing and dancing can also be incredibly powerful in huge numbers rather than small groups, but beware that the logistical challenge might be near impossible to orchestrate under occupation. Sometimes, there is power in a protest being composed of simply one person. One person in the middle of a large square, with the appropriate lighting and atmospheric effects to highlight the performative solitude of that act. Like someone incarcerating themselves in a fake jail cell in the middle of the town's square and refusing to get out of it for an extended period of time. Doing all of their daily activities, including shitting, in that jail cell. To communicate the extent to which they are being contained within the claustrophobia of being incarcerated in the daily life of This Place. Sometimes, the protest didn't need a person. Rather, it was better served as an installation of objects and texts that did not include a human presence.

STEP 3: GIVEN THE AGREED UPON FORM AND CONTENT, WHAT IS THE SAFETY PROTOCOL?

When there are incredibly large crowds that descend on the same place, at the same time, there is a certain power and safety that is less possible with smaller groups or an individual protestor. In fact, if someone did something absolutely alone, like the jail cell example described above, what's stopping That Place's armed forces from immediately removing them from the square? This is where one more layer of design comes in.

For example:

EXAMPLE 1: A large crowd could all clump together, like this.

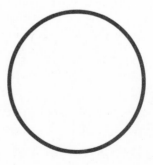

EXAMPLE 2: Smaller groups would need to form smaller clumps, but with a large cluster around their perimeter.

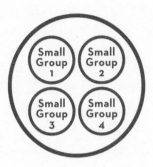

EXAMPLE 3: If the focus of the protest is one individual person, there would need to be hundreds of others forming concentric circles around that person to afford them the protection that they needed. Something like this.

So, once the form is decided, the safety component would enter the picture and based on whether or not the protest would take place under/outside curfew, the exact numerical configuration of the protective extra layers of people would shift.

THE GALLIVANT

Curfew does mean many hours inside the confines of a house. Unable to go out for fear of being caught at the security checkpoints or by soldiers on a stroll outside the formal checkpoints or being in the wrong place at the wrong time during a protest that breaks out where you happen to be. So yes, most of the time during a curfew, everyone is indoors and that's where you have to stay. But even in the harshest of curfews, there is an hour or so of a 'break.' An hour when particular neighbourhood shops open up, when people in that neighbourhood may go out in order to buy groceries or purchase medications or go to an ATM because they need cash to buy groceries or purchase medications or pay the labourers who need to be compensated for the work that they completed the day before the curfew was declared, and who now need the cash sooner than initially planned because they have to go back to their homes in That Place (given the tenuous condition of This Place). I'm sure you have something similar wherever you are.

During such breaks I love going outside the house for a walkabout. To complete errands, sure, but also because I need a breath of fresh air. Usually, I try to get two hours in the outdoors during curfew. If the "break" is only sanctioned for one hour, I know that I have to be extra careful about that second hour of outdoor exploration. If the "break" is sanctioned for two hours, I'm in luck and I can accomplish all the things on my list before having to head back indoors. I have made a list of places that I go to during the breaks, sanctioned or otherwise. I suggest creating a similar list for yourself.

(1) I make a grocery list by consulting everyone in the house. What they are craving to eat/drink that day, which we don't already have in our pantries-that-are-stocked-for-unexpected-and-expected-curfews. Even if there is no guarantee that I will be able to acquire the list of things that people at home are craving, I've found that everyone's eyes light up when they are making their wish lists. And for that light, for that glitter in the eyes of my mother and father and brother, I carefully make a list of what they want, knowing that I probably won't be able to get most of the things they are asking for. They know that too. It is a shared understanding of the illusions of joy that must be prized even through expected disappointment.

(2) Then, during the break, I go to the grocery store first. Being earlier than everyone else means that I can get any special item that might be limited in availability. Of course, getting there before other people is something of a task. Everyone has a break from curfew at the same time. Which means that everyone lines up at the shops at the same time. Unless they are super creative and manage to find a hiding place somewhere near the grocery store from which they can run up to the shop's entrance before anyone else has even left their home. But, to be fair, everyone is likely to have one of these hiding spots so that they can beat everyone else. So, any way you look at it, the lines are going to be a shit show. Regardless, the grocery store is my first stop. That way I can tell the folks at home that I have really done the best I could to get them the chocolate bar they are craving or the meatball that is the only thing that would satisfy their nostalgia for a time gone by.

(3) Then, I go to the ATM. Cash is hard to access in times like these and when most shops would not accept credit/debit cards during curfew—because of longer processing times—you have to make sure that there is currency on hand. Of course, that sounds easier than it actually is. Usually, ATMs run out of cash within the first five minutes of a curfew "break," because of the sheer volume that people want to withdraw to be on the safe side. So, making sure you have money from the ATM means carefully planning the breaks. On the first day of the curfew, go to the ATM *before* the grocery store. Make sure you get enough currency to last for a few days of groceries. Then, for the following days, you can go to the grocery store before all else, because you have the cash. If the curfew lasts for more days than you first withdrew money for, you'd have to use another break that prioritises the ATM rather than the grocery store.

(4) Usually, for me, just the ATM and the grocery store take an hour. Between the waiting and the catching up with neighbours and finding moments to chat with the people in the collective who ask for my advice on designing the next protest. The latter is the hardest: finding a way to talk about what we want to talk about with an army presence every five feet. We've developed coded speech in order to address these situations, of course, and have established a non-internet-or-telephone-based messaging system, but it still sucks to have to feel the claustrophobic army gaze even during the supposed break from claustrophobia.

(5) Time that is left after the errands is spent finding spots where protest check-ins can happen in a

more leisurely fashion. Most often, this means waiting till the shops close again after the break and sneaking back into the store of an owner who shares our particular political and ideological quest. Behind closed shutters we then plan our next protest. What have we heard about other neighbourhoods? What time should we hold our event? What would be the goals of this protest? What are we trying to achieve? And once those discussions lead to more clarity, I am tasked with designing the event—details that I would be in charge of sharing with the group during the next break. Yes, we always plan a protest during the first two days of a curfew being declared, despite not knowing how many days we might need to anticipate. And then, regardless of when the curfew actually ends, the protest can be executed.

Once the goals for the protest have been articulated on Day 1 of the curfew, I come up with design options:

a. Design Option 1, if the curfew continues on the day of the planned protest

b. Design Option 2, if the curfew is broken before the day of the planned protest

Finally, if there is any time remaining after the errands and the protest planning, I use my outdoor-time to go sit by the lake. Watching the glitter on the water always eases my spirit, and even though curfew means that this simple action becomes a huge luxury, I do what I can to make it happen. Sometimes I have to enjoy the water while hiding behind the trees on its banks, because the break was unsanctioned, but my outdoor-time-quota for the day had not been met.

Day 6

The Gallivant was probably the easiest of the strategies to follow.

The more time I spend under a self-imposed curfew, the more I wonder about the notion of time. What does time mean... how do we perceive time, and how do those perceptions in turn affect the ways in which we live our lives? How does someone who sees time as linear live life differently than someone else who sees time as being fragmented, or cyclical, or triangular...?

I've been sitting here for the last few days, trying to articulate how I see time. And while I can make no promises that I will agree with these ideas tomorrow, this is what I understand today. That time can be as slow or as fast as your mind decides it is. And because of that, yesterday, today, tomorrow are all useless concepts. Ultimately, what defines our approach to our days is the way in which we see the clock speeding up or slowing down. Are we racing against it? Are we flowing with it? Or is it simply immaterial? Can we control how we see time, and thus, how that seeing affects the way we make our decisions? Do I decide to take on this simulation/enforced house arrest because I see time as limitless? Am I willing to take this time to force myself indoors because I am not afraid of my time running out? What if I was more fearful? Would I reject the idea of such simulations that would cut me off from the outside world?

Like I said, it's all a bit blurry at the moment. A knotted roll of twine that includes a whole range of feelings and thoughts and responses.

I don't want to romanticise this experience. I am mining it. For nuggets of wisdom. For ideas that will inform my Curriculum. For inspiration. I still have no conception of what such experiences are like when they are not chosen. When they are forced.

I don't know so much, and yet, I feel like I know just a little bit more.

I don't know if I can make it to a week.

10:25 AM

▪ Still don't want to talk about it?

◆ No. I think we're getting closer though.

▪ To?

◆ To the right time to talk about it.

▪ You know this because . . . ?

◆ I just know it.

Change the subject.
Find something else to talk about.
Something that completely ignores this thing that you don't want to talk about.

What could we talk about?

Maybe politics is an easier topic area to deal with?

Nah. Not in the mood to be called an occupier again.
Not right now, anyway.

Ask about the updates on the wedding plans?
Nope.
You know there's been no updates.

He's been sitting here with you.

Ask about the weather?
No.
That's too obviously banal.

Ask for something more about his first love?
Dude. He died, remember?
Don't bring that up again.

Love . . . relationships . . . curfew . . . wedding . . . the wedding.

◆ Before I forget . . . since it looks like today's event is going to be cancelled, will you please finally explain the ritual to me now?

■ It really would be better for you to see it. The explanation would ruin the magic of seeing it live for the first time.

◆ Yeah but who knows when it'll happen now, no? And whether I'll even be there when it does?

■ You're thinking about heading back?

◆ Back?

■ To That Place?

◆ No, no. I'll call them later and if they tell me that the project's been postponed, I'll have to think about how long to wait for the wedding before heading back. Because who knows how long that could be. And if the project is on, I'll have to head to the cantonment the day after tomorrow anyway.

- Right. Right, of course. I forgot about the project. In that case you're probably going to definitely miss the wedding. Did I just say, "probably going to definitely?" Not a good sign when I so significantly lose my verbal skills. Anyway, the ritual I wanted you to see . . . It's one of my favourite rituals in the wedding festivities, you know? Because I think it's so evocative in its simplicity. One of the to-be-wed partners' families makes a huge pot of cooked rice. The family of the other to-be-wed partner brings over a particular mixture of spices that they make by toasting all the spices that they had in their home on the day that the two people agreed to get married. You know what I mean? Essentially, on the day that the wedding is confirmed or announced, one of the families claims the rice. The other family then has to make a list of all the spices that they had in their home on that particular day. Then, the day before the wedding, those spices are toasted and roasted and mixed together in different proportions—the way they are mixed together is up to the household making it. So, essentially, during this ritual, one household brings the rice and the other brings the spice mixture. They set a big ass pot in the middle of the room. All the members of the household that has brought the rice empty their contribution into the pot. The members of the other household then collectively pour their spice mixture onto the rice. Then the couple makes a big show of mixing the rice and spices together while everyone else sings the wedding songs. And finally, when everything has been blended, the partners feed a mouthful of that mixture to each other, before then feeding a mouthful of the dish to each member of both households . . .

- Feed, as in, with their hands?

- Sometimes. Sometimes the couple decides to use utensils. It's really up to the partners. They decide how they would like to make that happen. It's a chance for them to show what they're bringing to the other's family, so they're encouraged to think about how they'll share the food. They're encouraged to be creative in that task. They could decide to do the food sharing together, where both of them hand small amounts of the mixed rice to members of both households or they could decide to do it separately. They could do it the exact same way as each other or each member of the couple could have their own individual way of engaging with the other's family. All of these choices are part of what the couple wants to make part of their ritual. It's their way of communicating how their union is going to create ripple effects for their families. This one time I went to a wedding where one of the partners had the food placed on their body, their *naked* body, and the other partner's family had to eat off them. That was a particularly out-there approach.

♦ No shit. Seriously?

■ Seriously.

♦ Off their naked body?

■ Off their naked body.

♦ Wow. That would never have been allowed to happen in That Place! I can't believe that word on the street there is that y'all are more 'conservative' than we are!

■ I know, right? I mean the naked body thing is an extreme example, though. That wouldn't happen every day. To be honest, we were all a little taken aback when we saw that approach to the ritual. But the families had been prepared, obviously, it was just a surprise for the few of us who were invited to observe. I guess they didn't think we needed to be prepared if we were only going to be observers.

- That sounds fascinating. The ritual itself, I mean. Not this particular interpretation. That's fascinating too, obviously, but yeah. You know what I mean.

- Yeah. It's a beautiful ritual. Our bride and groom have not given us any clue as to what to expect. They say that the surprise is the whole point with their ritual, that each of them is going to bring their families unexpected joys and that's what they most want to say about the two of them coming together as a couple.

- Damn, I want to see what they are going to do!

- I'll try to take photographs for you . . . if it doesn't get too crazy.

- If you can, that would be phenomenal. I've never been to a wedding here . . .

\ \ \ \ \ \ \

- Is the spice mixture usually any good? It sounds pretty, I don't know, plain rice and a random mix of spices?

- That's the cool thing though. Within those parameters, each family gets creative, right? So, there are families who will boil the rice in milk, for example, rather than water, or they'll add one extra ingredient to the rice. That's technically bending the rules but, whatever. Similarly, the household that brings the spice mixture experiments with the elements, you know? They'll try to blend the spices in different proportions and push what they can do without adding anything else. People get really creative. Sometimes, when it seems likely that a wedding is going to happen, families will stock up on different kinds of spices a few days before the wedding is announced. Just so that they have more options for when the dish does need to be made!

◆ How are you all cooking the rice?

▪ Well, that's part of the surprise too apparently. We haven't been asked to help with the rice-making. My brother has decided that he's going to craft his own version to represent our family . . . I'm sure he has some cool, meta-explanation for why he's made that choice.

◆ That's not breaking the rules?

▪ Well, technically, sure. But it's a tradition. Traditions have to evolve. Otherwise, what's the point?

◆ Can I have one of those? I promise I'll keep you company later to buy some more!

> She pulls the cigarette out of the pack.
> She lights the cigarette.
> She takes a drag.
> She focuses on how she blows the smoke out.
> She focuses on the smoke and the patterns that it makes in the air.
> She looks at the cigarette and consciously decides to ash it.
> She watches the grey dust fall into the receptacle.
> She takes the next drag.
> She follows the same steps of the ritual.
> She watches her fingers twist and turn the stub as its light finally goes out.

- What a beautiful allegory. The two families bring different things to the table and the mixture of those things yields an entirely new creation that then feeds back into the families who brought the individual elements in the first place.

- There's that dimension to it, of course. But the layer that's particularly poignant to me is the historical . . . ummm . . . what do you call it . . . context? Framing? Whatever. So, apparently, back in the day, the ritual was not restricted to spices and rice. People used to make an inventory of whatever was in their kitchen on the day that the wedding was announced—like a full list, not just spices and rice but also meats and veggies and drinks and everything else. And then, each of the two families would bring one dish that was representative of their home. They could use whatever ingredients they wanted and be really inventive and creative with what they cooked. So then, when the families came together on the eve of the wedding, the mixture of the dishes would really lead to an explosion of tastes and colours and smells and textures. Over time though, the tradition has had to evolve. Families realised that many of their weddings would have to happen under crackdowns and curfews and there was no guarantee that what was available on the day the wedding was announced would be procurable on the eve of the wedding itself. So, the tradition evolved to include only spices and rice. Because all homes in This Place, regardless of curfews or crackdowns, are likely to have those staple goods. And even if your home happens to run out of something like rice or spices on the day before the wedding, you'll be able to borrow those things from any of your neighbours. The tradition *had* to evolve, essentially, to allow us to hang on to the essence of a ritual we would have completely lost if, you know, we were still forced to make these extensive dishes that we made in the past.

- Who changed the tradition? Someone specific? Or was it just like, you know, a gradual shift over time and no one knows who started it.

- Well, a little bit of both. We don't really know exactly who changed the ritual, but we do know when it happened. It was during the Golden Age of Revolution, when the revolutionaries encouraged a spirit of evolution, of not acquiescing to any limitations that might be imposed on our ways of life, so they started introducing these little evolutions where traditions and rituals that would otherwise have died out—because of how access to resources had changed over time—were articulated in a different way, you know?

■ Just help yourself to whatever you want, yeah? We're just going to have a quick family check-in to see if any new options have presented themselves. Maybe you should practice The Glaze! Or The Graze, even!

° Is she having something to eat? °

Yeah, she's fine. What are we going to do? Are there tunnels? ■

◊ Her parents are looking into it with some people in their neighbourhood. ◊

° I still think this is a terrible idea.°

▷ You've made your point, Mom. But it's my wedding and I have to try every possible option, no? Besides, we don't know if the tunnels are even an option yet. ◁

Okay, so we're still waiting. Why did we have to check in about it? ■

◊ Because her family wants to know if you have any contacts through your work who might also be able to look into this for us. ◊

Hmmm . . . ▪

▷ Do you? ◁

A couple of the folks I'm meeting later today
might have some thoughts. I can ask them? ▪

▷ Hopefully we'll have it figured out before then. ◁

Don't get your hopes up too much okay? ▪

▷ What? ◁

Just. It's a long shot. Even if there are tunnels, we
don't know how safe it'll be. Don't put all your
eggs in this basket. ▪

▷ It helps to have something positive to focus on. ◁

I know. But just don't make the hope so overpow-
ering that it's going to devastate you if it doesn't
happen. Keep a healthy dose of cynicism, okay? ▪

◊ We just don't want to see you deal with more . . .
shit than you have already had to deal with in
the last day. That's all. ◊

° It's okay, darling. It'll be okay. °

\ \ \ \ \ \ \

▷ I'm sorry, Mom. I know a sobbing groom
is the las—◁

° You have nothing to apologize for. We all need a
good cry sometimes. You just let it all out, ok? °

And so, he did.

Sobbing till he couldn't sob anymore.

Sobbing like there would be no tomorrow.

And like they always did when one of them had to take the time to sob, they sat with him.

Held him.

Without saying a word.

Many times, in places like This one, words are insufficient.

Many times, in This Place, the sobbing needs to be given its own time in the glitter.

- You're getting better at this.

◆ I am, aren't I? I can see how it helps.

- I've had years to perfect the technique. This is your first proper cur-few. Give it a few more. It'll become like second nature to you.

◆ Yeah . . . What's helping me a lot are the colours through the glitter. This weird thing happens as I fall into it, you know? It's like . . . the thing that I'm looking at breaks apart into its different, individual colour components, but instead of then existing as those individual colours, it's like the colours pass through the glitter and then they become almost transparent, translucent really, it's like you can see shapes in the colours rather than through the colours, and the shapes in some way resemble the thing that I was thinking about at the back of my head before even starting the glaze. Fascinating.

\ \ \ \ \ \ \

◆ What? Why are you looking at me like that?

- Have you decided how long you're going to keep doing this back-and-forth thing?

◆ As long as it's necessary.

- You don't mind the constant traveling and living out of a suitcase?

- That's the plan at the moment. I often wonder if I could live here.

- Just take the plunge and move here!

- Who knows, right? Maybe I could make it happen.

- What are you worried about?

- Honestly? Days like today. I don't know if I have the kind of strength and resilience that you all do. To put up with this. All of this. Day in and day out. For . . . you know . . . without a time limit.

- It's not the kind of thing you know until you're in it. You can think about it all you want, but you will not know if you can adapt to life in This Place till you're actually here and you have to live all of this like we do. It's amazing what a person can adapt to. How quickly this can all feel normal.

- Is that a good thing?

- It's a thing. Whether or not you want this to be your normal? That's a different question. Also, a question of—you know—

- Insane privilege. I know. It's the whole premise of my work too, isn't it? That with enough time and priming and willingness and effort, an individual's responses and ideas and behaviour and the very way in which their brain is wired, can evolve and change and adapt.

- Right. So just take the plunge and move here!

- You know I can't do that.

■ Because of her?

♦ No. Not because of her. It's too new for any decision about my future to be based on her. She's just . . . It's just a fun thing at the moment. The thing I wonder about is that all the resources that are there. In That Place. The money and the institutions and all of the other things that I can draw on to make my work here more effective. Living in That Place helps me maintain those connections and harness all that energy, you know? To make my work possible in This Place. In some way, maybe that's where I'm more useful too, you know? If I lived here, I think they—in That Place—would discount my work with so much more ease. "She doesn't even live here. Her sympathies are with This Place." But because I live there they can't claim that I have some agenda that ties me to . . . I don't know. As I say it out loud, I hear how weak those arguments are.

■ They're decent arguments. They just sound like a little bit of an excuse.

♦ I know.

\ \ \ \ \ \ \

■ Was that too honest?

♦ You know that's what I prefer. And you're right. It's a bit of an excuse. Moving here would be a big step and I don't know if I'm ready t—Is that the phone?

■ Let me see what's happening.

♦ Give me one of those smokes before you go?

Light.
Take a drag.

Can you hear what they are saying? Sounds like a whole lot of mumbling from up here. Well, there would be louder sounds if this situation was getting better. The mutedness could only mean that nothing was really changing in the situation. Right?

Ash.
Take a drag.

You need to make some time to sit down and plan the workshop. Well, maybe first call the commander to see if —No, she has this number in case of emergencies. She'd call if something had changed. Stop trying to procrastinate and just start getting the planning going. You know you need to do it at some point. What better time than when you have nothing else to do.

Ash.
Glaze.
Glaze.
Glaze.
Glaze.
Glaze.
Glaze.
Glaze.
Glaze.
Glaze.

◆ Was it them?

■ Yeah. No change in the situation, apparently. If anything, it seems to be getting worse in their part of town. The soldiers have started patrolling the neighbourhood now and everyone is terrified that they are going to barge in and fuck up all the wedding decorations in the house.

♦ Does it mean that today's event has officially been postponed?

■ Officially, not yet. I don't think they want to call it off unless absolutely necessary. Which it sounds like it is. But they don't want to call it for a few more hours. Even if we start two hours from now, we'll be done at a decent hour. That's probably what they're hoping for. A late start and less-than-ideal-but-doable finish time. That would be preferable, any day, to a cancelation.

♦ Is he holding up okay?

■ He's fine. Well, he'll be fine.

♦ Okay . . .

> *Is he spinning out?*
> *Fuck.*
> *Just be a good friend.*
> *Should I touch his shoulder?*
> *No.*
> *Just sit.*
> *Give him your focus.*
> *Just listen.*
> *Just be a good friend.*
> *Just listen.*
> *Just watch.*
> *Just witness.*

Glaze.
Glaze.
Glaze.
Glaze.
Glaze.
Glaze.
Glaze.
Glaze.
Glaze.
Glaze.
Glaze.
Glaze.
Glaze.
Glaze.
Glaze.
Glaze.

■ What were you glazing about?

◆ Just making a plan for the next workshop.

■ Day after tomorrow, right?

◆ Right, if all goes well. Who knows? Now with all of this going on. Maybe it won't happen. If they're out on patrols, there's no way they have the time or the mindset to be in a workshop with me.

■ It's probably when they need the workshops the most. Have you heard that statistic? That the suicide rate among soldiers spikes during the first twenty-four hours following patrol duty.

◆ Yeah.

■ What's the session plan this time?

◆ Well, with this unit, we are in the second section: the reframing phase. You remember that one?

■ That's the one about questioning orders? Before they do the simulation?

◆ Exactly. Asking them to reconsider why they need to blindly follow orders in order to be loyal to their nation. Reframing what it means to be a good soldier. That being a good soldier might actually mean being thoughtful, and critical, and having a mind of one's own.

■ I never thought you'd get this far with it! I still cannot believe the army is allowing you to do this shit with their soldiers.

◆ It's not the entire army. It's this one commander who is allowing me to do this shit. She's a badass. She keeps telling me that it's her passion to change things from the inside. That she joined the army to redefine what it means to defend one's nation. Can you believe that? I still can't believe that I found someone like her in an institution like that. I don't know how long it can last though. At the moment, she seems to be the only person here—of that high a rank—who is involved in this. I haven't met anyone else at the commander level or above who is thinking like this or who even knows the subtext to these workshops. But there must be others, maybe just not stationed in This Place. Otherwise, she wouldn't be so confident that she can get away with all of this. If she's not alone in this, then there's a chance of something shifting in the long-term. If she is alone though, once her time in This Place is up or her time in the army is up—whichever comes first—programs like mine are going to be fucked. Got to do what I can while she's still in there or make sure she eventually trusts me enough to let me into the bigger picture, to introduce me to her colleagues who are in on all of this with her.

▪ I'm amazed she still has a job.

◆ Me too. There's only two ways that's possible. Either she has really powerful colleagues somewhere in the military establishment or in the government or something like that. People who are protecting her and who share her ideas. Either that, or the higher ups don't understand what she is trying to do, and so she's getting away with it because of their lack of understanding. Even if she has some support in higher places, she's still outnumbered, right? In the establishment in general but also in This Place. So, she must be obfuscating the nature of the work in a really clever way. Otherwise, I feel like she'd already be in the process of a court martial. Maybe even arrest. They're serious about imposing their treason charges these days. So, I don't know the exact details, obviously—she doesn't really let me attend meetings with other officials. Probably for good reason. She's the only one who is in touch with me and then she relays information to anyone else who needs to know what I'm doing for like, I don't know, scheduling and programming purposes. But I did see this one report that she wrote up about the execution of section 1 of the Curriculum and she sent a draft of that document to me so that I could edit and add to it. Anyway, from that document I think I see the strategy that she is using. I think what she does is that she couches the work in all of these fancy words and terms and ideas. So, they think I'm doing some kind of therapy that helps the soldiers feel better. She's good at being so vague about this program that they have no idea what she's talking about. Like, she's calling it Somatic Pedagogy or something like that. Fuck if I know what that even means. And I think she articulated the rationale and purpose of this Somatic Pedagogy stuff as being about allowing the soldiers to "heal the parts of themselves that have suffered from alienation in This

Place" or something like that. And the cool thing is, she's not really lying. I mean, of course we're trying to address how soldiers deal with alienation. But she's making it sound like we're trying to breach the alienation between the soldiers and the local population here. But the truth of the matter is, the workshops are trying to heal the alienation within each individual soldier, from their non-soldier self. But saying that would get her in deep shit. So, she says the other thing. If she ever gets taken to court for this, I think it gives her plausible deniability. She could always say that that's not what she understood as happening. Lord knows, we've never even used the term 'deprogramming' in anything that has been documented about the project.

- Smart lady. And you trust that she's being honest with you? That she's being straight up about her motivations for supporting you in the execution of this Curriculum? What I mean is . . . how do you know that she . . . are you sure that she's not just using you to identify the weaker links in her ranks? You know, the ones who are less susceptible to their brainwashing? So that she can get rid of them or court martial them or whatever it is they do with the ones that don't buy into their particular brand of nationalism? Or, I don't know, she's heard about your Curriculum and wants you to implicate yourself in something treasonous before she . . . I don't know . . . You could go to prison for that kind of thing.

- I trust her. I'm taking many precautions too. In the beginning, I never even used the term 'deprogramming' in my conversations with her. And even when she and I spoke about all of this, we spoke about it through the reference of the Faraway Place, you know? Like, we both talked about how the Faraway Place has unique approaches and how we wondered if those ideas could apply here. Neither of us ever mentioned the term deprogramming in relation to our collaboration. Once we had sort of . . . established? No, yeah, established that we were on the same page, I insisted that we video record a conversation in which she explicitly identified herself and her rank and clarified her purpose. Like, why she wanted to collaborate with me. How she thinks the army needs to be dismantled and how that needs to be done by deprogramming soldiers.

- You recorded that shit?

♦ Yeah. Someone wise once told me to cover my bases, after all. You were right. I need to have some proof in case things go south. And she understands that I need to do that. To protect myself.

- So, in this recording she identifies herself and says what she is hiring you to do.

♦ Yes. It's a video recording so you can see her face.

- But doesn't that just put both of you at risk? If they find this video, they'll take you both out! I mean some of these high-ranking army guys are like a dog with a bone. They are vicious about anyone who says anything remotely against the army. If they realise what the two of you are trying to do . . . I just don't want anything to happen to you.

♦ You're right, the recording will not help with the army. If they find it, we're fucked. I mean, if they find out about what we're doing, video recording or not, we're fucked. The only reason I have the recording is the hope that if she tries to use the workshops against me in some way—like if she tries to use my work to get rid of soldiers who are more willing to question the army or something like that—or if she gets taken to court someday and tries to misrepresent how the program was set up and place the blame all on me, then I will have some kind of evidence to show why I went along with her. Why I worked with her. The truth of the matter is though, if word about this gets out, nothing is going to be enough to save our skins. And if she tries to throw only me under the bus, I'll use the video to take her down with me. That's all the video is. Some kind of mutually assured destruction so that I'm not the only one who can be implicated because I'm the one who's running the sessions. It's . . . it's been bizarre. She's had an IT guy check my internet presence and make sure that all references to my University work around deprogramming are just off the internet. I feel like I'm some kind of spy.

■ Right. Well, it sounds like she knows how to handle the situation you're in, and I hope you're both able to keep flying under the radar. But . . .

◆ I know. It's uncharted territory.

■ It is. It also isn't. Anyone in This Place—wherever they are from— faces grave consequences for the—You remember that journalist that you were talking to the last time you were here?

◆ I heard what happened to him.

■ Right. And all he was doing was being 'moderate.' All he was saying was that This Place, That Place, and the Other Place needed to get their shit together and talk it out. But because of that, he was branded a moderate by the radicals. And when he gained attention overseas, the homegrown revolutionaries called him a traitor. And to the government of That Place, he was a successful local intellectual who was not doing them any favours on the global political stage *and* he was becoming a household name. If a man like that could be taken out—

- I hate to say this, but it's different for him. The stakes are higher. The risks are riskier. It's different for him.

Because he's from This Place. ■

- Because he's from This Place.

\ \ \ \ \ \ \

- So, remind me again how the Reframing section works? I'm sure it's changed quite a bit since I've read it, no?

- Yes and no. It's changed in so far as I've gotten a lot more specific about each part of the Curriculum. What each section entails, what the expected outcomes are, how to measure each exercise's effects, and all of that. I've tried to build in more safeguards to protect myself and the soldiers. But otherwise, the overarching pedagogy and goals, those are pretty much the same as they were when you last read the document.

- How many sessions do you have allocated for the Reframing section this time?

- For the Reframing part alone? Four eight-hour sessions.

- And that'll be enough?

- I'm not sure. You remember last time, when I tried the Reframing section with the previous batch, they gave me two eight-hour sessions and that was definitely not enough. So maybe four eight-hour sessions will be better? I don't know. I keep telling them that rather than giving me eight-hour long days they should give me fewer hours per session but more sessions overall. It's a constant scheduling challenge with them. Apparently it's easier to give the soldiers long chunks of one kind of activity rather than spreading those hours out over other days and, you know, interrupting other kinds of training that they have. Not to mention that there are always unpredictable days when the soldiers are sent on patrol and cannot attend the classes. I'm just taking what I can get at the moment. I need more data about the effects and impacts of my sessions before I can make stronger claims for the kind of schedule that would be ideal for the Curriculum. I don't know.

- One person released themselves last time, right? Because of the Curriculum?

◆ Two.

- Two soldiers released themselves from the army because of your sessions? That's fantastic!

◆ Two soldiers. Out of sixty.

- Well, it's still two fewer soldiers on our streets. Two fewer people in the armed forces who are fighting in a war that is definitely not in their name.

◆ For the first attempt yes, I suppose a 3 percent success rate is . . . something.

- Hey. First time or not, anything better than 0 percent is something. They say that every soldier who is deployed here ends up killing at least 3 people a year, injuring approximately 100 more and psychologically affecting close to 421 This Place citizens.

- How the hell do they get such specific numbers?!

- Point being. Two fewer soldiers in This Place means that you are saving more than a thousand people from death or some kind of injury in one year alone! That's fucking fantastic. By any standards.

- I'm still curious as to how they landed at those incredibly specific numbers. That's kind of amazing.

- I don't know. It was this human rights agency that spent about five years collating data. They were trying to gather the kind of information that would really make the international community sit up and listen. If each soldier deployed here negatively affects more than five hundred people each year, imagine the consequences when That Place deploys hundreds of thousands of soldiers to this region, right? They're decimating an entire population. An entire civilisation, even. Essentially, with these numbers, there is not one single person in This Place who does not either die or get physically or psychologically injured because of the soldiers' presence here. I wish they would come up with similar kinds of statistics about the fighters. How many laws and policies have changed since the fighters started advocating violence? They claim that they have increased success rates compared to nonviolent protests, but I really don't see the numbers to back it up. Or even, I don't know, how many protests happen in This Place every year versus how many policy meetings occur related to the issues addressed in the protests. I suspect that the numbers will tell us that both violence and nonviolence have been ineffective in causing policy-based change. I think there's also likely no link between the number of protests that are held and the policy meetings that happen. Those people aren't even listening to the people on the street. Lord knows that I could use some of those numbers in making my work more effective. Or helping me justify to the fighters and revolutionaries how my design work can strengthen the efficacy of protests. Even in that data collection, the centre remains That Place; that kinda shit frustrates me. I know why it's important to study the army and its impacts on the local population, but even the way in which the study is structured centres the soldier from That Place. Not the five hundred civilians from This Place that each of those soldiers negatively impacts in a year.

♦ Maybe you should find a way to get those numbers yourself? Develop a decentred, decolonized way of generating the kind of data that would help the fighters of This Place?

■ I've tried that. Tried to design a methodology that would account for the sheer number of variables that are included in something like a protest, right? But because the whole structure of protest is designed to be unpredictable, and because people are constantly on the move to avoid any kind of surveillance by That Place's authorities, it becomes impossible to put systems and strategies in place to generate data and conduct research. I wish they had those fancy agencies here, you know? The ones that invest shit tons of money into tracking people and into developing technology that tracks people and all that jazz. But that shit never comes to war zones. Well, not to the civilians who are living in war zones. I'm sure the army has access to crazy advanced mechanisms for collecting data about our protests and fighters and revolutionaries. But obviously, they will only use the tech to serve their own purposes. Nah, the cool technological stuff will never be available to us. We only get the feel-good-kumbaya-types who are trying to teach us how to weave baskets for reconciliation.

♦ Tell me how you really feel.

■ Ha. Sorry. I hate those fuckers. You know, the do-gooders who come here and pretend that they are not in a conflict zone. Who pretend that we don't need any high-technology developments or things in that realm because we're the poor victims of war who will be happy with the scraps that are thrown our way. That we just need feel-good measures rather than strategies that will allow us to control our own fate. Those sorts of people. Man, they frustrate me. If you're going to come to This Place, you need to understand that EVERY-THING needs to be contextualised by the occu—war. I don't even know if I'm making sense. It just makes me mad. The centering of the oppressor in a story about occup—war.

♦ You can say that damn word.

▪ That's the whole point about a war, isn't it? It seeps in everywhere. You can't come here and talk about how you'll teach farmers how to set up credit unions and act as if the agricultural and banking structures are not intricately linked to the hierarchies That Place creates in This Place. It's all interconnected and it's frustrating when people try to ignore that by pretending like . . . like . . . I don't know . . . like an economic Band-Aid is somehow going to fix a bleeding wound that is mired in politics. I don't even know how I got on to this particular train of thought.

Find a point.
Focus.
Find the blur.
Glaze.
Glaze.
You need to get back to work and continue the planning.

Glaze.
Glaze.

Glaze.
Glaze.
Glaze.
Glaze.
Glaze.
Glaze.
Glaze.
Glaze.
Glaze.
Glaze.
Glaze.
Glaze.
Glaze.
Glaze.
Glaze.
Glaze.
Glaze.
Glaze.
Glaze.
Glaze.
Glaze.
Glaze.
Glaze.
Glaze.
Glaze.
Glaze.
Glaze.
Glaze.
Gl—

- Do you want me to let you get back to work?

■ Mom will bring something up for you in a little bit.

♦ She doesn't have to worry about that.

■ You can say that all you want. If she decides you need some nourishment, you're going to get it whether you want it or not.

♦ Sounds like my mom.

■ Done for the day with that? Or still editing?

♦ I think I'll be editing and refining for a lifetime. This time it's just little tweaks though. There wasn't really enough bandwidth last time for me to be able to develop the content in any significant way. Are you ready for your planning meeting this evening? Do you have to prepare something for it beforehand?

■ Not today. Today is the first day of the curfew so that usually means that it's a strategy meeting. I'm a fly on the wall in this one. Just listening to what people want to do and achieve in the next week's protests. Tomorrow I'll have to sit down and come up with some design options. You're coming with me, right?

♦ What!

■ You said you would go outside with me to replace the smokes you've been bumming!

◆ Yes, I'll go with you to replace the smokes, but I don't think it's a good idea for me to go to the meeting, no?

> Maybe if you change the garment? If you do, you'll totally look like someone from here. I can tell them you're a distant cousin or something. Oh, come on, I'm kidding. I would never put you, or them, in that position. I think you should come along. We'll tell them who you are—leaving out the army part—let's just call you a teacher or a researcher. Actually, I'll tell them first and see how they feel. You can wait outside. ■

◆ That sounds better.

> Yeah. Usually that wouldn't have been necessary. That kind of prior clearance. But given the weight of what's happening right now, I think it's better to be extra careful. ■

◆ What if the army stops us while we're outside?

> They're not going to do anything to you. You're one of them, as far as they're concerned. ■

◆ You know they're going to give me grief about what I'm doing here when they told all the tourists and visitors to leave last week.

■ Tell them the truth.

- That I'm here to deprogram them?

- No, that you're here for a wedding. Of course, it wouldn't hurt to drop it into the conversation that you know that commanding officer lady that you spoke about.

- Name her? Wouldn't that be risky?

- Nah. It would just be name dropping. They're not going to try to contact her or anything. They've got too much on their plates. But knowing that you're well-connected would help them just let us on our way instead of just, you know, making things difficult by asking thousands of questions that they don't need to be asking.

- When should we go?

> She needs to see what it's like during curfew to truly understand the importance of her work. Why the deprogramming of soldiers is so fucking necessary. She needs to see how robotic they become when they are out patrolling the streets during curfew. When they don't even look at us in the eye, because to look at us in such a way would be to recognise us as human, and, in situations like curfew, they seem to want to treat This Placers as being something other than human. That way, the soldiers can keep us at arm's length. They can keep us at a distance. So, when they have to come into our homes and rummage through our belongings and take away our people, they don't feel so bad. Because they don't think of us as human . . .
>
> Maybe witnessing that would give her some more

ideas for the Deprogramming Curriculum. Some sort of contextual, firsthand insight that would help with some aspect of what she was going to undertake with the soldiers.

Yes, she definitely needs to go out with me today. We'll have to be careful. I'll have to make sure she wears the thing to camouflage herself.

But yes, she needs to go out with me today.

- Why don't we go after you've had a snack?

◆ Should we go downs—

- Nah. Mom said she wants to chat for a while. She feels like she hasn't had the time to be a good hostess.

◆ It's a curfew. On her son's wedding. She doesn't need to worry about what kind of hostess she's being.

- You know that and I know that. But it's important to her. Just roll with it, okay?

◆ Okay.

- And be prepared for intrusive questions and comments.

◆ Right.

- Don't be surprised if she asks you how much money you make.

◆ Sounds like the kind of thing my mom would find a way to bring into the conversation not-so-subtly.

- Sounds like our families have some things in common.

\ \ \ \ \ \ \

- Have you called them yet? Your parents?

◆ Not yet . . .

- Don't you think you should?

◆ Yes.

- But?

◆ I know what they're going to say.

- That you should get out of here as soon as possible?

◆ Yeah. And that's not a conversation I want to get into. Certainly not on the landline in front of everyone.

- I can ask them to give you some privacy if you want?

◆ In a bit. Let me get some food in me first. Then I'll call them. I need the extra fuel.

- Speaking of fuel—

      ° Thought you might need some replenishment. °

◆ Yes, please, Aunty! Thank you so much! I would have been happy to come downstairs. You didn't have to—

It's one flight of stairs. ▪

° Ignore him. Happy to do it. I was getting bored
downstairs. His father is busy with the neighbour and his brother doesn't want to do anything but talk on the phone. °

Have they had the kid yet? ▪

° That's what your dad is trying to figure out. He's
over there now, talking to the boy's parents. °

It's not like they're going to know anything . . .
there's no landline in the house. ▪

° Yeah, he's trying to get them to come here, so
they can answer the phone if their son calls
with the news. °

Ah, now I understand. ▪

◆ This is delicious, thank you! And here I thought you might be running low on supplies.

You know she would never let that happen in this
house! Give me the shopping list, Ma. We'll go
out once she's done refueling. ▪

◆ Yup. Just give me a few minutes.

° Don't be ridiculous. You can't take her out there
on a day like today. °

She'll be fine. ▪

◆ I'll be fine.

° I think it's a bad idea, but I know better than to argue when young people make up their minds about something. Be careful. °

. . .

° What have you been up to, sitting in here all day? °

◆ Your son has been teaching me how to glaze. So, I've been practicing that to pass the time.

° Ah, yes. The famous glaze. He has tried to pass on that skill to all of us. °

It's never worked for you all because you refuse to surrender to The Glaze. ▪

° Right, that must be what it was. Nothing to do with you staring at us and yelling, "JUST FALL INTO THE GLAZE" the entire time. °

◆ He was a better teacher this time! It actually worked for me.

\ \ \ \ \ \ \

◆ What's your glaze equivalent, Aunty?

° My glaze equivalent? °

◆ Yeah. He was telling me that every person in This Place has their own approach to dealing with curfew. Some strategy like The Glaze to pass the time. What's yours?

° I clean. °

◆ You clean?

She cleans. Obsessively. ■

° He's right. It's a bit obsessive. That's what I was doing downstairs. To be completely honest, I didn't come up here because I was bored. I wasn't bored at all. I just came up here because I was trying to see when I could get in here to clean. Maybe when you both go to the market. Which I still think is a bad idea for her, by the way. °

You are ridiculous, Mom. ■

° So is glazing, but it works for you, right? Anyway, cleaning really helps me. I set aside a certain number of hours, each day of curfew, for each room in the house, you know? And a different cleaning task for each of those days, just to keep it interesting. On the first day I dust all the rooms and make sure that each room gets about an hour of attention. On the second day I sweep each room in the house. The third day I mop each room. The fourth day I clean the cobwebs. The fifth day I polish the furniture. You know how it is. There's always so many tasks that need to be completed to really get all the grime out. And what better time to do all of that than during curfew. °

◆ Wow.

° I came up with this strategy when I was eleven
or twelve or something like that. Around the
same age that he was when he discovered the
whole glazing thing. I think that's sort of the
time when most people in This Place find the
strategy that works for them, if they ever do.
The ones who don't have a much harder time
keeping it all together. Everyone needs a strategy to deal with curfew. I think I landed on
cleaning because it helps me feel like I can control something in all the madness of the shutdowns and patrols and all of that. And it makes
the house look good. Uncle cleans during non-
curfew days but obviously, there's more time on
days like these for me to really get into it. °

Don't miss how she psychoanalyses what she does
while she is talking about what she does. ■

° What else do you expect from a psychology pro-
fessor? Speaking of which, how are you doing
with all of this? It's still new to you, no? °

◆ Yeah . . . Well, yes and no. I've been here during crackdowns in the
past, even the odd curfew. But I've never been in a wedding during
curfew. Well, not literally a wedding, but you know that I mean.
That part is definitely new.

° This is your, what, seventh or eighth year
visiting us? °

◆ Seventh, yes.

° Were you here last year? °

◆ When that commander was killed? Yeah, I was here.

° So, you know all about curfews. That was a bad one. °

◆ Well, I wouldn't say that I know 'all' about curfews. My project got suspended immediately after the curfew started so I left like, I don't know, the day after it was declared.

° The project with the army people? °

◆ Yes.

° I don't know how— °

Don't start with that, Mom. ▪

◆ It's fine.

° She can speak for herself. You don't have to intervene in her defence! °

◆ No, it's fine, Aunty. I know it's controversial. You know what I'm trying to do though, right? I told him that he should share it with you all, so that you are aware of what I do when I'm here.

° Yes. He mentioned something about deprogramming or something like that. °

◆ Yeah. I'm trying to figure out how to deprogram That Place's armed forces and get them to behave differently. To not be, you know, how they are now. Maybe even get some of them to leave the army.

° And do you think it'll work? °

◆ I hope it will. But it will take time. Years. Decades. And that's if people like the commander I'm working with now are able to fly under the radar, while also getting more people in their ranks and higher to believe in the need for the deprogramming. If not . . . well, it's just a question of time before all of this is shut down and it becomes one more well-intentioned effort that goes to naught.

° I appreciate the intentions. I think it's a wonderful and creative way of trying to figure out how to change the shit show that is This Place. But, to be honest, I don't think it'll work. °

Come on— ▪

° Let us have a conversation, please! She's an adult. If she wants me to stop talking about this, she can tell me. °

◆ Really. It's fine. Sometimes I don't think it'll work either . . . But I'd love to know why you think that's the case.

° I think they are too far gone already. The soldiers. The army. That entire institution. Those people. They chose to join the army. They *chose* to do that. And even if some of them felt like they had to choose it for practical reasons or if they felt forced into it because of family pressure or whatever, they're still choosing to continue to. To go on. However pressured one feels into doing something, there's a limit, right? After which you cannot do that thing anymore before it goes against everything you stand for and believe in? But these people . . . Whatever their reasons for joining the military, after being stationed here, after seeing what happens, after seeing how some of them choose to shoot at us. How some of them choose to torture us. How some of them choose to rape us. Even after seeing all of this, they choose to stay. That tells you their character. That they can stand there and watch, as people like them, who represent the same institution and country and government that they do, that they can stand there and watch as an entire civilisation is decimated. Unjustly. At that point, doesn't it stop mattering why they joined the army? Doesn't it also tell you how far gone they are? That they are willing to be part of—I know you know all of this. °

She knows all this. ■

° Right. So, my point is this. If they've already agreed to go along with the machinery, despite seeing the horrible damage that their institution is causing to This Place, is there any hope for them to change? Can your work actually rewire what their brains and bodies have come to accept as their truth? °

◆ I don't know.

\ \ \ \ \ \ \

◆ Did you have a favourite teacher in school, Aunty?

° What? °

◆ Just humour me for a moment. Did you? Have a favourite teacher in school?

° Yes. My English teacher in the tenth grade. She was fantastic. °

◆ And until you had that teacher, how did you feel about English as a subject?

° I was indifferent to it. Hated it on many days. °

◆ And after her?

° I was still indifferent to it. °

◆ What made her your favourite teacher then?

° Well, I was still indifferent to the subject, but I didn't hate going to English class as much as I did before having her as my teacher. °

◆ And is it possible that, because of her, you even enjoyed the class a little bit more, you paid a little bit more attention? Maybe even learned things that you wouldn't have earlier, simply because you happened to be paying attention?

° Sure, that's possible . . . Okay, I see where you're going with this. But—Never mind. Let's talk about something else. °

◆ No, tell me!

° Look, I know how one person, one teacher, the right teacher, can really make a student open their eyes. Make them engage with aspects of knowledge that they never knew they never knew. But the difference is, I used to see this teacher every day, for months, before I realised that she made English classes more enjoyable for me. Before I realised the range of things that I had to learn from her. Before I was willing to let her ideas even remotely affect me. You are here for what, one month a year? You see them for a few hours a day. Do you think that's enough time to, you know, deprogram them or whatever? °

◆ It's not enough time. You're right. But at this point, it's all that the commanding officer can get me without calling too much attention to the work. At the moment, while I'm away, she does small work-shops—as much as she can get away with safely—so that there is some continuity. But we've been talking about what it would look like for me to be here, you know, for the long haul. And to see if we can frame the classes as everyday sessions that the soldiers would need to do. For months at a time. Maybe even a year. If anyone can pull it off, it's the commander. That lady can spin these things like nobody's business.

° Long haul. So, you'd move here? °

\ \ \ \ \ \ \

° Why are you both looking at each other like that? °

No, no. We were just talking about that, that's
why . . . ■

♦ Yes. If it seemed like things could really grow. And . . . I don't
know . . . If we're able to get the kind of results we're hoping to get,
and it seemed like there would be ways to make the work happen
on a regular basis . . . I mean, there would be a lot to consider but . . .
yes. Yes, I think I would love to move here to see if this could actually grow into what I think it can become.

° And what is that? °

♦ What, Aunty?

° What do you think it can become? °

♦ In the long-long term . . . When I'm dreaming big, my hope is that
there will be no more reports of human rights violations by the soldiers who are stationed in This Place. No more disappearances. No
more tortures. No more women being raped. No more killings at
protests. Soldiers who, at the protests, are really there to protect the
protestors from an unpredictable occurrence of violence. Soldiers
who listen to the people in This Place and try to understand them as
individuals. Soldiers who listen to their conscience and their ethical codes without following orders that they do not understand or

agree with. I hope that there will be no more suicides among soldiers. That there will be an increase, each year, in the number of soldiers who decide to leave the army and to return home to That Place to pursue other dreams. To consider a life outside the military establishment. That there'd be, consequently, fewer people joining the army because there'd be more people on the outside, telling them why they shouldn't. Eventually, in the long-long-long term, I hope the armed forces will cease to exist. And That Place redefines itself as a nation.

\ \ \ \ \ \ \

° Those are wonderful things to hope for. °

Right. ▪

◆ But I also know that as soon as I get even remotely close to one of those hopes, I'll either be arrested or killed or exiled.

° So why do it? If you know how risky this work
can be, why do it? °

◆ Because it seems worth doing. Even for the smallest, most infinitesimal chance that it could truly shift a pervasive status quo, it seems worth doing.

She hates you.

No, she doesn't.

This is just a conversation.

Stop overreacting.

Focus on the food.

Eat.

Comment on it.

Say something.

The silence is killing me.

I wish it didn't have to be like this.

I wish it didn't have to be like this.

I wish it didn't have to be like this.

I wish it didn't have to—

◆ This is delicious. Thank you.

What's your prediction, Ma? How much longer before we can get back to the celebrations? ■

° Oh, I don't think it's going to happen today. I've been telling him to start looking at the calendar for new days in a couple of weeks from now. That's the soonest that I think we can expect things to ease up. Anything sooner would guarantee more rescheduling. °

◆ You think this will last for that long?

° Longer, probably. °

◆ But I don't hear any protests or anything. The roads seem empty. Isn't it the case that the protestors are out if things are really bad? I remember hearing voices of protestors during the entire time that we were under curfew last year, and that was a bad one.

° Well, that's only been the way of things for the
last ten years or so. The number of protestors
who are out on the streets as a symbol of how
bad things are getting out there. But this, on
rare occasions, and the last occurrence of this
kind of gravity took place over twenty-five
years ago, it's the silence that serves as a cau-
tionary note. As an indicator that bad things
are about to come. When something of the
magnitude of this policy change happens and
things are quiet, it's not a good sign. It usually
means that serious trouble is brewing, This . . .
this change is not like anything we've seen before. I heard that they've started placing all the
party leaders under house arrest. °

Yes. Well. That's to be expected isn't it? ■

° They don't want people to have their own leaders to look up to at a time like this. God forbid
our leaders give us some guidance on how to
respond, after we have lost every last bit of our
sovereignty. °

♦ I can't believe they're doing this. I feel like I need to apologize for
my government in some way . . . No, seriously. I know it sounds
foolish but I just—It feels like all citizens of That Place are culpable
when something like this happens.

° No. Come on. What are you going to do? Fight
your government? You'd end up in jail or dead.

Just like the rest of us. It was just a question of
time before this happened. I just didn't think it
would happen so suddenly. °

It hasn't really been sudden, has it? We've been
seeing this coming since the last election . . . ▪

° I suppose that's true. °

♦ I keep hoping that something miraculous will happen. That somehow, suddenly, they'll realise that this is a bad idea and just . . . stop.

° This is the time when we need all your deprogrammed soldiers! You should have started
your work with them a few years ago! °

♦ I know, right?

She hates you.	*I wish it didn't have to be like this.*
No, she doesn't.	
This is just a conversation.	*I wish it didn't have to be like this.*
Stop overreacting.	
Focus on something else this time.	*I wish it didn't have to be like this.*
The weather maybe.	*But it is. And you need to find a way out of the spiral.*
Or the condition of the glitter or something.	*Inhale.*
Comment on it.	*Exhale.*
	Inhale.
	Exh—

° Your parents must be incredibly worried. °

◆ Yes.

° They know that we're having an internet black-
out, right? °

◆ I'm sure it's on the news . . .

One can only hope that we even make it to the
news in That Place. ■

° Have you called them yet? Updated them on things? °

◆ I've been putting it off. I know. I'm an asshole.

° They're never going to let you come here again. °

◆ It's not like they have any say in the matter really.

\ \ \ \ \ \ \

° Why do you keep coming back here? To This Place? °

◆ There's no rational reason. It just happened. I was looking for ways
to do this deprogramming work and thought long and hard about
where this work would be most useful. But once I came here, once I
saw how the army acts here, This Place has become . . . everything.
It's been slow going though. It took a few years before they'd even
let me work with the soldiers.

° So, what did you do on the previous trips? °

◆ Meetings. Lots and lots of meetings. Some with the army but many others too, trying to understand the lay of the land and how the work might even function if it was done here. That's how the two of us met.

° Do you tell them all the truth about what you're looking to do? The people that you meet here? °

◆ Of course not. Only a handful of people know the reality of the deprogramming work. Others know that I do workshops and things but they under—They don't ask too many questions and I don't volunteer any information.

° I hope no one has been following you . . . °

Come on— ■

° You know that's a possibility! °

◆ No, you're right. I'm trying to be as careful as I can but . . . it's not like I can be invisible when I'm here. I think people know where I go. They don't know exactly what I do but I'm sure they have their suspicions . . . I mean, we take all the necessary precautions. An unmarked vehicle picks me up, takes me to a hotel which has an underground passage to the training centre, which is some distance from the official base camp of the cantonment. So, there is some cloak and dagger stuff to all of it, but I'm guessing that just like the army knows where many of the revolutionaries' hideouts are, the revolutionaries and fighters know that there's some link between that hotel and the army cantonment.

° I'm sure someone has seen something or has some suspicion . . . °

◆ I don't know. No one has asked me anything about it directly. Only the two of you. But you're among the few people who know.

She's just concerned about you.

She is looking out for you as someone who is close to her son.

As someone that she has some kind of affection for.

She's just concerned about you.

Just focus on that.

I wish it didn't ha—

Stop it.

Inhale.

Exhale.

Inhale.

Exhale.

Inhale.

Exhale.

Inhale.

Make it stop.

Make it stop.

Make it stop.

° I don't think you should move here. The risks would be much higher if you lived here. At least now, just before you get on someone's radar, you leave and then something else happens that gets everyone's attention. They forget till the next time that they see you. And by then, things could have changed so much that you're no longer anywhere close to their radar. But if you lived here, if and when you got on some-

one's radar, they would be able to focus in on
you. There'll be fewer distractions. Or even
if there are, you'll be on their radar in a more
permanent way, which would make you more
at risk. It would increase the risks for everyone
you know as well, right? Because if you lived
here and they saw you. If you moved here, with
the work that you do, the risks would be expo-
nentially higher. Not only for you, but also for
the people in This Place who are in your life.
Like us. °

Don't— ▪

° You have to acknowledge this. I'm not saying
anything that both of you don't know. If this
project with the army becomes official and
you are going to be visiting the hotel and the
training academy more often, sooner or later
someone will figure it out. And they'll get word
to the revolutionaries and the fighters, who
are not known for being patient and doing the
research, you know what I mean? Because if
they bothered to listen to you, and truly seek
to understand why you go to work with the
army? Hell, some of them will probably want
to support your work however they can. But
that's the thing, right? We all live in such a
heightened state for so much of the time that
seeing someone from That Place go to the army
will immediately be construed a certain way.
Because, historically, that's what such occur-

rences have meant. Betrayal. Espionage. They
have no reason to want to understand why you
do what you do. So, once you're on their radar,
well, we're all fucked. You, because you're from
That Place and you're working with the army.
Us, because we're hosting someone from That
Place, who works with the army of the government occupying us. °

This might not be the ti— ▪

◆ Are you saying that I shouldn't have come to the wedding?

That's not what she's saying. ▪

◆ Don't speak for her.   ° Don't speak for me. °

° I am delighted that you're here. We are all delighted that you're here. We know how close
both of you are and having you at our son's
wedding is incredibly important to us. °

◆ But?

° But. The wedding has been postponed. The laws
have changed. The stakes are higher. From the
day after tomorrow you are going to be working
with the soldiers almost every day, if I understand correctly. Were you planning to continue
to stay here then? °

Mom . . . ▪

◆ No. No, I wasn't. I was going to move into army housing tomorrow in any case. To prepare for the workshop. I hadn't thought about what to do if the wedding got pushed.

Right. It's all happening quite quickly. ▪

° I'm not trying to make you feel uncomfortable
or unwelcome here. I hope you know that. °

◆ Of course. Of course, I do.

You don't have to say that. ▪

◆ No, seriously. Of course, I know that you're not trying to make me feel unwelcome. You've all given me a home in This Place, and I know that you wouldn't be saying all of this without very good reason. I wondered how long it would be before this project with the army would begin to affect my relationships with people from This Place. I guess I'm getting a crash course in that.

° I wish I could tell you otherwise. That it didn't
have to be this way. That it could be something
different. °

◆ I know.

° Look. What you're doing, if it works the way
you want it to work, it could be fantastic.
Incredible, revolutionary, even. It is work
that could be so important in the future of
That Place and This one. But, if any part of it

backfires . . . If any of part of it gets out to the
wrong people on any side of the divide, you
won't be bearing the risk alone. °

I think you've made your point. ▪

◆ You absolutely have. I totally understand. If the wedding is postponed and happens when I'm still in the area, I just won't come.
That's all.

Don't rush into a decision. ▪

° I think that's a good idea. °

Wow. Neither of you are paying attention to a word that
I'm saying, are you? ▪

° No. Because you're biased and you're not thinking clearly. °

What's that supposed to mean? ▪

° You know exactly what it means. °

\ \ \ \ \ \ \

° Has he told you yet? °

◆ What?

No. ▪

° Seriously? °

No, it's not my story to tell. I didn't want to say
something that you wouldn't be comfortable with. ▪

° I appreciate that. But I think she needs to know,
don't you? °

I . . . ▪

◆ I don't need to know anything that you don't want me to know.

° I think you should know. Just so that you can
better understand why I'm coming down so
hard on all of this. °

\ \ \ \ \ \ \

° Uncle is not his biological father. °

◆ Whose?

° His. °

Mine. ▪

◆ Uncle is not his biological father?

° No. °

No. ▪

◆ Okay . . .

° His father was someone I met when I was very
young. And very naïve. °

◆ Right.

° You know I dabbled in journalism, right? Right
after college? °

◆ Yes, I think I knew that. Yes.

° My first job out of college was as a correspon-
dent for *The Times*. I was young, excited. Very
sure that I was going to change the world with
my writing. So, for my first article, I decided
that I was going to do what no reporter in This
Place had done. I decided that I was going to
interview a highly ranked official in the occupying forces. °

◆ Wow. That must have been incredibly risky.

° Yes. Yes, it was. But we have a family member
who used to be in the army . . . you know how
it goes. He set me up with this interview. An
exclusive interview. This guy was high up in the
establishment and a journalist from This Place
hadn't had the—I already said that. Sorry. It's
not a story that I talk about very often. °

◆ You don't have to—

° I want to. °

\ \ \ \ \ \ \

° The room was bare, sort of. There was a desk
in the annex. A narrow couch and a large table
in his office. A bar next to the couch, with a
few different bottles of alcohol. The walls were
grey and the whole entire building smelled
like concrete dust. Like the building was being
renovated or under construction or something.
He hadn't told me that. That the building was
under construction. That the construction
crew had left for the day. That his secretary
had left for the day. That the building would be
empty, except for the two of us. If he had told
me these things, maybe I wouldn't have gone
there. Maybe I would have asked a colleague to
go along with me. Maybe . . . So, I went to his
office and we began with a tour. He showed me
around his office, let me know that everyone
had left for the day. Made sure to show me the
drawer in his desk where he kept his gun. Of-
fered me a drink. °

Should I ask a question?
To prompt the conversation?

No. Just keep your mouth shut.
And sit here.

She will continue the story when
she is ready to continue the story.

Focus on her.

Keep the energy on her.

Be a good listener.

Be a good witness.

You're a badass, Mom.

You're a badass.

I'm just going to sit here and
look at you and give you all
the energy that I can muster.
So that you feel the moral
support.

You're a badass.

You're a badass.

You're a badass.

You're a badass.

You're a badass.

° Not much you can do to defend yourself from a
high-ranking army official who tells you that
they have a gun and that they know how to use
it if you don't do what they want you to do. °

Fuck.   *Fuck.*

Fuck.   *Fuck.*

Fuck.   *Fuck.*

Fuck.   *Fuck.*

Fuck.   *Fuck.*

Fuck.   *Fuck.*

Fuck.   *Fuck.*

Fuck.   *Fuck.*

Fuck.   *Fuck.*

Fuck.   *Fuck.*

Fuck.   *Fuck.*

Fuck.   *Fuck.*

Fuck.   *Fuck.*

Fuck.   *Fuck.*

Fuck.   *Fuck.*

Fuck.   *Fuck.*

Fuck.   *Fuck.*

Fuck.   *Fuck.*

◆ I'm so sorry.

° Me too. He is the only good thing to have come
out of it. Him and Uncle, of course. I cannot
think of too many other people in This Place
who would have agreed to marry someone who
was carrying a child that was not theirs. °

◆ Yeah. That's . . . that's something.

° Especially when other people in This Place . . .
even the revolutionaries and the fighters . . .
were quick to pass judgment on what they
called my 'love child' with someone from the
other side. This made me a traitor in their eyes,
of course. One cannot sleep with the enemy. °

◆ But it wasn't your choi —

° They wanted me to get rid of it. Him. As proof
that it hadn't been my choice. "If you really
didn't want it to happen, why keep it?" They
couldn't see that I coul—I just couldn't do it.
And I have never ever regretted that decision.
But when I didn't just get rid of the baby, they
said that it was because the sex was consensual.
That I was a traitor who wanted to escape to
That Place and was willing to sleep her way
there. Of course, they paid no attention to
the fact that if that was indeed true, I would
have been on the next plane out of here. That I
would be in That Place with him. But of course,
reasoning doesn't really work with some folks.
And when I tried to get them to see the logic,
they said it was because I had brokered some
kind of financial deal with the officer. That he
didn't really want to be with me anyway and
when he realised that there was a baby, he paid
me shit tons of money to stay away from him . . . °

◆ Fuck.

° Indeed. °

\ \ \ \ \ \ \

◆ When did you find out about this?

A long, long time ago. It was never something
that was hidden from me. It's just not something that we bring up too often because, you
know, eventually, after some time had passed
and Mom and Dad got married . . . I think
people actually forgot about all the brouhaha
that had occurred before then . . . ■

° Right . . . the same people who gave me all that
shit actually had the audacity to come to the wedding and talk about what a blessed union it was. °

Motherfuckers. ■

\ \ \ \ \ \ \

◆ Thank you. For sharing that. I . . . I don't know what to say.

° Look, he trusts you. That's why I wanted to
tell you. But it's also why we need to be extra
careful with you now taking on work with the
armed forces. Our family already carries something of a burden . . . The reputation of being
associated with That Place comes with a lot of
repercussions in This Place. °

◆ I completely understand.

° You don't know this yet, but we've already had
to field a number of queries from people about
why someone from That Place is coming to the
wedding. The bride's fathers were also a bit . . .
concerned. But we were able to allay their suspicions and fears because we know how much
he trusts you. And because of that, we trust
you. But that was before all of this . . . °

\ \ \ \ \ \ \

◆ I'm so sorry.

° For? °

◆ It must be so hard for you to have someone from That Place in your
home after . . . after . . .

° Don't be silly. You're not that army officer.
You're a young person from That Place. My
fight is not with you. °

◆ But . . .

° We live in a war zone. We need to be extra
careful about who we let into our lives. Those
simple choices can change everything. °

◆ I know. I understood your concern even before you shared all of this—
but now, now I understand even more. Thank you for telling me.

° I'm glad you know. I would have hated for you
to leave here tomorrow thinking that this was
about you, personally. It isn't. Please know that. °

♦ I know.

° And promise me you'll be really careful, okay? °

♦ I will.

° I really don't want anything to happen to someone who matters as much to my son as I can
see you do. °

\ \ \ \ \ \ \

♦ I probably need to go call my parents. Make sure they know I'm
okay.

° Of course. Uncle should be back by now. He'll
help you use the landline. °

She knows how to use a landline, Mom. ■

° Right, of course. Well, if you need any help, Uncle is downstairs. Or just come get me. Please
tell your parents that we send them our best. °

◆ My parents send you their best, too.

Good. How are they? ▪

◆ Worried. Flipping out. The expected.

They want you to leave here tomorrow? ▪

◆ Yup.

Well, you can't expect them to be any other way.
They are your parents. It's a . . . yeah. They will
worry. ▪

◆ Right.

\ \ \ \ \ \ \

♦ They want me to call them every twelve hours to give them an update.

That sounds reasonable. ▪

♦ Well, they first wanted an update every two hours.

Good negotiating skills. ▪

♦ I've had a lot of practice over the years.

\ \ \ \ \ \ \

Do you still want to go out? Get some of the groceries? ▪

♦ Sure. Yes. Let's do that. It'll be nice to go outside for a bit. We better stock up on some smokes.

\ \ \ \ \ \ \

◆ You're sure this is ok?

Yes. ■

◆ I just don't want to—

Stop. It's fine. If it's not, I'll tell you and we can
turn around immediately. ■

\ \ \ \ \ \ \

◆ I don't think I've ever seen so many checkpoints in one neighbourhood.

That usually means they're preparing for a patrol. ■

◆ Fuck.

\ \ \ \ \ \ \

You ready to talk about it yet? ■

◆ No . . .

Okay. ■

\ \ \ \ \ \ \

◆ But we need to.

Right. ■

\ \ \ \ \ \ \

◆ I think I should head to the cantonment tonight.

Tonight. ▪

◆ Yeah.

The workshop doesn't start till the day after tomorrow. ▪

◆ Right. It's just a day earlier than scheduled . . . I called the commander after calling my folks and they're fine with me coming tomorrow.

You don't have to leave so quickly. ▪

◆ You heard your mom.

Yes, and she's— ▪

◆ She's right. It's too risky. Even this, us being seen out together like this, it's risky.

\ \ \ \ \ \ \

You don't have to leave tonight. ■

◆ I know I don't have to leave tonight.

Good. ■

◆ I think I want to though.

You do. ■

◆ Yeah.

Okay. ■

◆ It's too hard. To be around you. To be around this.

I know. ■

◆ But after hearing what she said . . .

I know. ■

◆ It's impossible.

I know. ■

\ \ \ \ \ \ \

After you left, Mom said that maybe we would be
really creative and figure out a solution. ■

♦ She did, huh. I can't think of something creative that would also
allow you to continue to live in This Place. Safely.

Exactly what I told her. ■

♦ Right.

\ \ \ \ \ \ \

So ... ∎

\ \ \ \ \ \ \

◆ Maybe someday . . . we'll have that epiphany. And figure out that creative solution.

Maybe. ▪

◆ And that day . . .

We can see where we're at. ▪

\ \ \ \ \ \ \

◆ Right.

Right. ■

WHAT IT BECAME

I know hiding notes in your luggage is juvenile, but this is all happening way too quickly and I need to do something because you're leaving in a few hours, and I know that I'm not going to have the wherewithal to say anything, so I'm hiding this note like a fucking adolescent.

Don't be a stranger. Please.

Even if we never figure out a way to be more than what we are now, what we are now is beautiful. Inspiring. Breathtaking.

It's not something we should lose just because we cannot see a romantic future together. Romantic futures are not the pinnacle, remember? You told me that. There are so many different kinds of pinnacles in this world, and we'll build one that's all our own.

A pinnacle that's ours. Just ours.

Stay in my life, okay? Be it from This Place. Or That Place. Or Any Place.

You, in some form, in my life . . . that's all I want.

I just got your message—when did you send it? How did the chat with the Commander go? Are you back in That Place already? When are you planning to come back?

Nothing much to report here. Not things that I can write about, anyway. Beautiful new designs that I'll have to wait to tell you about till all the surveillance mechanisms reduce.

We're still waiting.

Still hoping there will be a wedding soon.

Thank you for the note. I found it the day I got here. I just needed some time.

I hate this.

I knew it would come to this eventually, but I hoped we'd have more time to . . . something.

I keep replaying—no.

I'm going to keep this about work.

You know the rest.

They've allowed my sessions to go ahead, but I honestly don't know if it makes any sense to implement the program right now. Every single one of these soldiers is burned out. They're on back-to-back shifts because of the curfews and the patrols and all their free hours have been booked up by me.

I don't think it's healthy for them to not have any downtime. It's making them less engaged participants with me, and I'm terrified that it's making them worse soldiers on the streets.

I'm trying to schedule a meeting with the Commander to suggest that we delay the Curriculum until we have a better sense of how this crisis will evolve. It's probably going to take a few months. Years, even.

Your prediction that today is unlike-anything-that-came-before seems to be shared by many here. There's a palpable tension in the air. One that feels different from every-other-time-that-came-before.

There won't be more to say till the chat with the Commander happens. Besides, there's some kind of commotion going on outside and I better go see what's happening.

Yes, this is partly an excuse to stop writing because I still feel awkward as fuck.

Anyway, who knows when this message will even get to you.

Are you ok? This is the longest you've gone without some type of communication.

I've added some new strategies to the Guide because of this curfew. Want to see them?

Now I'm worried.

I'm giving you two more weeks, and then I'm calling your parents to check on you.

I spoke to your mom this morning. She told me.

Why didn't you call? We could have helped. We could have tried to help.

I'm so, so sorry. I hope you're not blaming yourself. Everyone in This Place is on edge and there could have been no way to predict that what happened would happen.

I understand your desire for distance. For space. For silence. Even from me.

I hate it. But I understand.

Whenever you're ready, whenever that may be, you know where to find me.

I just heard about Aunty. I'm so sorry.

I'm lying. I didn't just hear about her. I heard more than two weeks ago. It's taken me that long to be able to write this.

I'm lying again. I've actually written many versions of this in the last two weeks and it took all of those unsent messages for me to finally decide to send this one.

I'm so, so, sorry. For your loss. For disappearing. I'm sorry about all of it.

I fell into that clinched trap. The longer I didn't respond, the tougher it got to make a move, and somewhere along the way, it got easier to stay quiet. To pretend to forget. To pretend to move on. To pretend that my time in This Place was a phase that I've outgrown. Or lost. Or relegated to part of a past that I no longer want to talk about.

There's so much I need to say. Excuses. Truth. Memories that feel like fiction. I don't think I know the difference anymore.

I thought leaving you was going to be the hardest part of that trip. I still remember how it felt to pack my bags that night. I still remember the smell of your neck as we hugged goodbye. I still remember the yellow shirt that helped me see you till the jeep turned a corner. I remember the driver looking at me through the rear-view mirror, worried, because I was sobbing like a child. I remember wanting to turn back. To come running back and say, "Fuck the odds. Let's do this thing!"

When I left you that day, I told myself that the worst was over, and that I was headed toward more clarity. More purpose. More . . . something. I found solace in telling myself that I was about to make some kind of breakthrough with the Curriculum. I was on the brink of something. The verge of an epiphany. I was going to revolutionise education, soldiering, fuck, I was going to blow up the whole concept of the military establishment. I was going to do that. I look back at that time now and cannot believe how much I believed in, well, everything. Anything. Myself. The world. My place in it. There was this euphoria that I recall... it made the glitter look like diamonds. A glorious, euphoric, I-am-exactly-where-I-need-to-be belief that made everything else easier to handle. It made leaving you easier to handle. It made the loss of the concept of an "us" easier to handle.

I didn't expect to spend days in a cell not knowing if I'd ever be able to go home again. I didn't expect that soldier to turn the gun on himself. The Curriculum was supposed to encourage questioning and imagination and a healthy scepticism of authority. It was not supposed to lead to this. No. None of that was supposed to happen. It was not supposed to be that way. My people, my home... this could not be it. This could not be the way in which... I can't do it. I still cannot do it.

Even after all this time I can't find a way to talk about my time in This Place during that curfew.

All I've been able to do is make changes. To where I am. To who I am. Changes that make breathing more bearable.

I am saying some of this as an excuse. In the hope that compassion might get the better of any rancour you might be holding onto. But for the most part, this is all there is to say. I am not who I was when we last saw each other. And even though I miss her terribly, this is who I need to be now.

I am so sorry about Aunty. I am so sorry for whatever I might have unleashed upon you.

I am so... I don't know. That's all I've got.

Mom often asked about you. Even a day or two before she was taken away from us. Even after all this time.

We talked about time as we sat under the weight of that curfew. Remember? The idiosyncratic, personal, collective, and cultural approaches to time that shape our lives. Beliefs that shape the choices we make—the ways in which we understand the choices we make—as we build our pasts, presents, and futures . . . So, in one sense, it has been a long time. But in another, what is time anyway?

No, I'm not under the influence of any substances.

I met one of your soldiers the other day. I say "your" because she told me that she'd been part of one of your training sessions that year. The year of that curfew. I met her as we were setting up for a protest outside the University a couple of months ago—we saw a soldier approaching us. That action in itself should have been a clue. SHE came to US. I don't think I've ever seen that happen on the streets. Usually the commanders call protest leaders to their offices, and even that only happens IF they deem the leaders important enough to be spoken to. Never have I seen soldiers, commanders, or any member of the occupation's industrial complex, voluntarily engaging with fighters on the ground. The soldier's very approach should have been a clue that she was one of yours.

She talked to us for about half an hour before the protest, as we were setting up. Asked us what we hoped to achieve. Why we thought we needed to go out on the streets. She asked about the way in which we'd designed the protest—I'd written something like a script for a play, where different groups would read the narratives we've collected over the years. Overlapping histories. Overlapping voices. And at the end of the performance, the groups would—all together—raise a demand for the Board of Education to revisit the official history curriculum in the schools of This Place and That Place. You're credited in our materials, by the way, for being one of our most committed data gatherers.

Anyway, the soldier came over to us, and with that small gesture, the atmosphere changed. What would have otherwise quickly disintegrated into a shouting match suddenly became a conversation. After her chat with us I saw her go back to her battalion and tell them what we had discussed. "We'll stay over there," she came back and said to us, pointing to a spot much further out than where they would have usually stationed themselves. "We don't want to interrupt. If someone in your team starts a confrontation with us we'll have to do something, but hopefully you'll see that we're here just to, well, we've been told to be here to keep things calm, so here we are."

The protest that day was still a manifestation under occupation. We were still there under the gaze of a military presence. There was still surveillance. There were still armed people with weapons. There was still an inescapable hierarchy of power in which the soldiers assumed the top of the pyramid. The occupation didn't go away because of that soldier's actions, but, it sure as hell made the space feel different. If something like occupation could embody 'respect'—however antithetical the two concepts might be when placed alongside each other—this might have been it. If all soldiers were like her, maybe occupations themselves would become obsolete? Wishful thinking, I know. That's how much hope this soldier inspired in me.

That day felt different. It felt like the soldiers were transparent about their doubts. It seemed like they were being honest about their uncertainty around having to be at the protest and having to carry out their jobs in order to keep them. It was almost as if this acknowledged doubt made the soldiers more willing to hang back, and to step in only if they absolutely had to. Rather than stepping in before they needed to. Which, as you know, is what has been the norm in This Place.

At the end of the protest the soldier came back to us. Told us that she had learned a lot from hearing the different voices in our performance. Shared what she had learned about This Place when she was young. She even said, as a quiet aside, "If more people knew about the complexities to all of this, maybe we wouldn't have to be here anymore. Maybe then I could go home to my wife."

I had to ask her then. I had to ask if she knew you. If she had participated in one of your programs. And of course, she had. Her whole face lit up when she spoke of you and the ideas that your short time together had sparked for her. Yes, she did mention what happened with that soldier, but for her, his actions didn't define the battalion's experience with you. If anything, what that soldier did, made her see why your work was so necessary.

She asked when you were planning to come back.

I tell you this in the hope that it will spark something. Perhaps hearing about this soldier will give you a push? A push that, even if you don't admit it to yourself, you want? A push that you need?

Whatever happened that day, however many lives might have been affected by that cadet's action, it's not on you. You changed something—someone—for the better. And with that accomplishment, you saved more than a few lives that may have otherwise been lost in today's protest. That's something. That's more than something.

It has been a while since that curfew, hasn't it? A while that sometimes feels like decades, and at other times, like days.

They're married now. I'm testing out new designs. Dad is trying to rebuild his universe.

We're all grappling with what it means to live in a world without Mom.

Just like This Place, we're all same same, but different.

There are so many things that need to be shared and discussed and debated and mulled over and considered and ripped apart and put back together. But all those things will have to keep for another day. For now, there's only one thing I want to say.

Your fire, your spark, that's what makes you, you. Your belief in ideals that others deem irrelevant, even foolish. Your struggle, every single day, to find a purpose that takes you out of your Self. Your fight to keep taking steps—even when a step is more like a crawl, even when a step might take you backwards rather than forward. These are the qualities that make you who you are. And whatever life might have unleashed upon you, I don't think that core changes. It cannot. It physically cannot. Can it?

Maybe your fire is no longer about deprogramming soldiers. Maybe it's no longer about This Place. But I know you. I. Know. You. And I know that there is some Thing, in some Place, that is calling to you.

You once told me that opportunity knocks only once. And if you're right, the only way to know if it's opportunity that's knocking is to open the door every time you hear the slightest sound.

Consider this message a sound. Please open the door.

ACKNOWLEDGMENTS

Doug and Mila: for being the ground beneath my feet.

Lata, Dinesh, Nikhil, Lisa, Jennifer, Subarna, Rachel: for the eternal encouragement.

Mary Krienke at Sterling Lord Literistic: for her unwavering faith in this book; for understanding and accepting my idiosyncrasies; for being such a gracious and generous interlocutor to the complex world of publishing.

Alyea Canada, Carl Bromley, and everyone at Melville House: for taking a risk that many publishers wouldn't.

The organisations (that can be safely named) that have consistently supported my practice, research, and writing: the United World Colleges, Wellesley College, New York University, the University of Cape Town, the Watson Fellowship, the National Theatre Institute, the Ensemble Kashmir Theatre Akademi, The Company Theatre, Never Again Rwanda, Open Book Publishers, McFarland Books, Vernon Press, and Bombaykala Books/Curato.

Those who came before, whose words have provided inspiration and solace: Arundhati Roy, Salman Rushdie, Sarah Kane, Griselda Gambaro, Ngũgĩ wa Thiong'o, Tony Kushner, and Manuel Puig.

Those who have taught me: in Guatemala City, in Srinagar, in Mombasa, in Harare, in Pune, in D.F., in Ahmedabad, in Santa Fe, in Belfast, in Kigali, in Dimapur, in Cape Town, in Lira, in prisons, in IDP camps, in rehearsal rooms, in kitchens, in _____, in _____ , in _____ , in _____ .

The many who cannot be named. Because sometimes, in some Places, names can cause a whole lot of trouble.